Devil Water

A Chase Gordon Tropical Thriller

Douglas Pratt

MANTA PRESS

For Ashlee

1

The skin covering my right knuckle ripped as I rapped it against the diesel engine for the fourth time. That last bolt holding the fuel pump just wouldn't give.

When the designers of the Tartan drew the plans, they didn't leave a lot of room to work on anything. The diesel was situated underneath the companionway steps, meaning that the only way to access it was to remove the stairs and crawl into the compartment. "Crawl" was a bit misleading. My head and one arm barely stretched between the edge of the opening and the Perkins engine. Sure, there was plenty of room around the engine to store tools and parts but being able to access them was an entirely different prospect.

The fuel pump crapped out sometime last night. Normally, that's just a giant pain in the ass, but when you are hundreds of miles from shore, it becomes a bigger problem.

Add to that the eerie calm where *Carina*, my 40-foot Tartan sailboat, found itself. The wind died completely yesterday afternoon, leaving the boat afloat in near glass-like water. I was just out of the Gulf Stream, so the current barely moved, and with no wind, there were no waves to toss the vessel back and forth. A good thing, given I had to pull the fuel pump. At least the still waters made the job a little less difficult.

My weight shifted off my calves so I could turn a little more. With a new angle, I slipped the socket onto the head of the bolt and pushed against the ratchet's handle.

It budged.

Not a lot. Just a microscopic amount.

I put every muscle in my arm against it. The handle rotated a half an inch.

"Come on, you son of a bitch," I hissed through the sweat dripping off my face.

The lack of breeze made the 87 degrees in the midday sun feel closer to 103. On an average day, the wind, even a tiny gust, will keep me comfortable in the cabin. Now it was becoming an oven.

I pushed again. The ratchet twisted as the bolt released its grip on the engine. My hand rocked the handle back and forth until my fingers turned it freely. With what seemed like zero dexterity, I pulled the bolt free, feeling the weight of the fuel pump drop into the palm of my hand.

Currently, Carina floated somewhere between Grand Cayman and Belize. When I left Georgetown on Grand Cayman, I was looking at a four-to-five day relaxing sail to Belize City. That was almost three days ago. The wind had slowed, which is unusual in this area. Old sailors often talk about hitting a dead calm. In some parts of the world, these pockets of calm, windless sea occur all the time. In the Caribbean Sea, it was unheard of. At least as far as I knew.

It would have only been an inconvenience if the fuel pump hadn't locked up. When one is a few hundred miles at sea, there aren't a lot of places to pick up extra boat parts.

I stock several duplicate parts for such an emergency. Alternators, starters, and, of course, fuel pumps. Still, it's a lot easier to swap out engine parts at the dock.

Once I wriggled the pump out of the compartment, I rose to my feet, letting the blood get back to all the right areas.

Since the weather wasn't pushing me to get the motor running, I replaced the steps and climbed into the cockpit. The sweat dripped down my chest. I'd stripped my shirt off an hour ago. The main sail was up, but with no wind the canvas was luffing. I pulled the jib sail in earlier. It was just hanging limply, and I worried that if the wind picked up suddenly, it might catch a railing and rip.

A coil of rope hung on the stainless-steel railing at the stern of Carina. I unfurled it with one hand, caught the loop at the end in the palm of my right hand, and dove into the calm, blue water.

While there wasn't any wind at the moment, the sea can play some wicked tricks. I didn't want to find a sudden gust race up and carry my boat away from me. It was, after all, a long swim back to shore. That's what the rope is for. A tether to keep me close to my home.

The water was refreshing after baking in the engine room. The salt water burned my knuckles, but the old wives say it's good for scrapes and cuts.

I rolled onto my back and floated on the surface for a few minutes. When I'm away from land, I often anthropo-morphize the ocean. She will talk to me, soothe me, and scream at me. The sea often offers a different emotion. Stormy seas are filled with rage. Rolling waves embody lust and passion. Today, though, she only offered peace. It's a silly thing for a big, bad Marine to ponder, and if I told Jay, or anyone I served with, I'd be dealt a fair helping of ridicule and laughter.

Of course, right now, it was just me and the sea. And my other love, tied about 50 feet from my hand.

My stomach grumbled a bit after I had cooled off. Lunch would need to wait until I finished swapping the pump. There was still some Mahi in the fridge from the one I reeled in a few days ago. I started fantasizing about how I might prepare the leftover fish, and I settled on fish tacos with some of the mango and pineapple I diced up.

Hand over hand, I pulled myself back to *Carina's* stern and climbed the ladder. If I wanted to eat, then I needed to get that spare fuel pump back on.

If it hadn't been for the stifling heat, the lack of wind wouldn't have bothered me. Even the motor wasn't a big concern. I wasn't on a schedule. That's pretty much what most of my life is like. At least when I'm at sea.

If I'm stateside, I try to refill my cruising kitty by slinging drinks in West Palm Beach. However, the Manta Club, where I work, is in the middle of a major renovation. I could have stuck around and picked up a few shifts at other bars, but I didn't like the hassle. The Manta Club is only 100 feet from where I dock *Carina* at the Tilly Inn and Marina. In fact, it takes up a corner of the Tilly Inn's first floor.

If I went somewhere else, I'd have to figure out how to get there. That would mean having to get a car, or at the very least, a bus pass. All that seemed too sedentary for my tastes. I don't like staying put very long. There were enough funds in my piggy bank to keep me going, so I finished up some minor repairs on *Carina* and set sail to Cuba.

As I stepped into the cockpit, I paused, hearing something in the distance. My eyes searched the horizon for a speck on the water before my brain registered the sound from above. A few miles southwest, a dot moved across the sky. Those little dots were the only sign of human life I'd seen in the last 48 hours. It wasn't a commercial jet, but once I noted that, I lost interest.

I climbed down the steps. The spare fuel pump was under the starboard settee, so I pulled the cushions off and shoved them into the v-berth. As I opened the compartment, I heard a pop in the distance. It sounded like a gunshot.

My curiosity pulled me back on deck, where I scanned the sky for the plane. It was closing in on my location, but it was lower in the sky. A plume of smoke streamed from one wing.

Quickly, I jumped down the stairs and retrieved my binoculars. When I zoomed in on the jet, I saw a steady stream of black smoke. The nose was dipping and rising, as if the pilots were struggling to keep her level.

"Oh shit," I mumbled as I studied her trajectory. She was heading in what appeared to be a straight line toward me.

There are hundreds of square miles of vacant ocean, and they planned to land that bird on my boat. My hand reached back through the companionway to grab the microphone for the VHF radio. Airplanes communicate on a much higher frequency than my radio would operate, however, on the off chance I reached someone, a water rescue could be mounted.

"Mayday, mayday," I announced into the microphone. "This is the sailing vessel *Carina,* calling. There is a plane in distress."

I pushed a button on my chart plotter before continuing. "I'm at 18°42'37.8" North 84°12'02.9" West. The aircraft is smoking and losing altitude."

I waited for a few seconds and repeated the coordinates again.

No response.

One more time. Still no answer. It didn't surprise me. There wasn't another boat around. The range of the VHF radio was only around 30 miles. Someone might pick it up farther away, but they'd need a larger receiver. If they did, it was doubtful I'd be able to hear their response on my radio.

The plane was coming down fast. It veered toward the west, no longer on a direct path toward me.

I went into action. The lines holding my little wooden dinghy on the davits hanging off the stern released when I untied the knot. *Beth*, my 10-foot tender, dropped to the surface with a splash.

When I released the cam cleat holding the main halyard in place, the line zipped through the hole in the cleat as the main sail dropped. It wouldn't go all the way down unless I took the time to pull it down. There didn't seem time for that, so I hoped that the weather would hold, and the wind wouldn't arrive while I was gone.

The port locker under the cockpit held my scuba gear. I hadn't planned to use it until I reached Belize. No point in 10,000 feet of water. Unless one has to enact an underwater rescue.

My hand gripped an air cylinder and pulled it free. A compressor in the locker let me keep the tanks filled, and I connected it to a regulator before attaching it to the buoyancy compensator device, or BCD. The BCD acted like an inflatable life-jacket, keeping me afloat.

A crash pulled my attention up from the gear as I watched the plane strike the water about a mile from me. As the nose dove through the surface, a splash preceding the concussing wave.

Hurriedly, I lowered the BCD and tank into the dinghy before scooping up a mask and fins and tossing them into the bottom of the little wooden boat. I grabbed my dive knife, a six-inch blade secured in a sheath that strapped to my calf, and a weight belt with about 20 pounds of lead weights. I have a tendency to float, which makes descending a grueling ordeal.

My feet hit the floor of the tender and rocked it violently. As I started the 15-horsepower motor, I shoved the bow away from *Carina*.

Beth usually only reached about 10 to 12 miles per hour when pounding through rough seas, but with the flat, calm water, I hoped I could push her faster.

The V of the bow cut through the water with ease. This kind of calm reminded me of water-skiing in the man-made lakes of North Arkansas. As a kid, we would often spend weekends camping at one of the lakes situated among the Ozark Mountains. The best time to get out behind the boat was first thing Sunday morning. My sister, a devout church-going girl, swore it was the devil trying to keep us away from Sunday school. She called it "devil water."

Today, I assumed it wasn't the devil behind it. The smooth surface let *Beth* run wide open. With no waves to slow her progress as she tried to bash over the crests, she sped up close to 20 miles per hour.

Smoke continued to billow from the wing that was sticking out of the water. The front half of the jet had submerged. Along the surface of the water, flames blazed around the plane. Jet fuel fed the flames, creating a circle of about 20 to 30 feet around the aircraft.

I cut the engine and studied the wreckage. The tail seemed intact, but there was no way to see how the nose survived the crash. There could be survivors, but at the rate the rest of the plane was submerging, they wouldn't last long.

Then I saw the palm of a hand pressing against the second to last window.

2

Where was the door?

I stood on the bow of *Beth* and tried to figure out where the door was on the jet. The safest route was the most direct, and I didn't want to be forced to swim under the plane because I chose the wrong side.

Pieces of fiberglass and metal floated through the flames. How long before the flames ignite the entire plane? Would that even happen? Perhaps the fuel tank had already submerged, and while it was under water, there was no way to ignite the fuel. I wasn't sure if jet fuel burned under water. It wasn't something I'd considered in the past. Regular fuel didn't tend to. At least as far as I knew. No oxygen meant no flame. Right?

The body of the jet sank a little deeper as I tried to decide how fire worked. No more time to waste. I donned the BCD, pulled my fins over my feet, and slipped the strap of my mask over my head. With the regulator in my mouth, I rolled off the side of *Beth.*

The only way to get to the plane was under the flames. I sank below the surface and pedaled my feet until I was 15 feet down.

The water was crystal clear. The right wing was visible; the engine under it was black and contorted as if it exploded.

I located the door about 40 feet forward of the wing. By now, the nose was dipping lower in the water. In a few minutes, the plane would be perpendicular to the surface.

Trapped air in the aft section was keeping the craft afloat, but the water was pushing all that air out fast.

My fins propelled me down toward the door. I checked my depth gauge. The needle hovered just over 50 feet.

A levered handle opened the door. I exerted all my effort as I pulled against the increasing water pressure. After nearly a minute of struggling, the door swung open a crack. That was the hardest part. Once I created a gap, the ocean helped push it open.

Cushions, cups, and assorted trash swirled around the dark cabin as I swam through the opening. The hand had been in the rear window, which meant I had to go up.

It felt like an odd sensation, reminding me of some cave dives I did in the Mediterranean, as I swam toward the surface in the rear of the plane. My hands used the backs of seats to climb up. I didn't want to inflate my BCD unless

I had to. There might be a need to rush out, and I didn't want to wait for the BCD to deflate if there was no time.

My head broke through the surface. Debris floated all around my face. After a second, I oriented myself. The water had reached the last six rows of seats. A lavatory door hung open over my head. I guessed it was at least 25 feet from the surface to the back of the plane. It seemed like a lot of space, but I doubted it would take long for the air to leak out.

In the back row, a woman clung to the back of a chair. Her head burrowed into the seat cushion, and her sobs echoed off the metal walls and the water. Her blond hair hid her face, and I figured she had already surrendered to fate.

"Are you hurt?" I shouted up after spitting the mouthpiece out.

She didn't move.

"Lady!" I screamed. "Are you hurt?"

The blond hair moved as she lifted her head. Her face showed confusion as she tried to register the frogman appearing out of nowhere.

"Who are you?" she asked.

"Not now," I insisted. "You need to jump down here to me. I can get you out of here."

Her head rocked.

"It'll be okay," I promised. "We just have to hurry."

"I can't," she told me.

"I have an extra regulator. You just have to breathe. I'll take care of the rest."

She trembled, staring at me as I lifted the spare mouthpiece.

"Drop down to me," I ordered. "I'll get you out."

After another 20 seconds of wide-eyed staring, the woman finally nodded her head. Her fingers gripped the headrest as she inched toward the edge.

"Just let go," I encouraged her.

Her chin made a nearly imperceptible motion that might have been a nod. The poor woman was in shock. There wasn't much I could do for that, certainly not inside a sinking plane.

Her feet hung over, but she still wrapped her arms around the seat. My feet kicked to push me up, but she remained out of reach.

I know little about planes beyond flying them. My uncle taught me to fly on a couple single-engine crop-dusters, but I never got a license. Structurally, they are built to endure the pressures of altitude, but I wasn't sure how that differed from the pressures of the ocean.

My biggest fear at the moment was that something would rip off the plane, destroying the integrity of the craft, evacuating the remaining air, and dropping the thousands of pounds of metal toward the ocean floor with me still in it.

"Come on," I urged.

The woman looked down one more time and let go. Her squeal reverberated off the walls of the plane. She splashed into the water, and I grabbed her.

"Hold on to this," I told her as I put her hands on the seat just below the water.

She shook in my arms but obeyed.

"Here." I put the octopus regulator in her mouth. "Just breathe through your mouth, okay?"

Her head nodded.

"Don't hold your breath. Just breathe. I'll guide us out."

"Okay," she mumbled through the regulator.

"Hold on to me. I won't let you go." My regulator slipped between my lips, and I sank below the surface.

With one arm wrapped around the woman, I used my left arm to pull me down by grabbing the headrest and shoving us deeper. As I passed each row, I repeated the thrust until we reached the door.

My depth gauge read 60 feet now. We'd lost 10 feet while I was inside. The woman squeezed her eyes shut, and she didn't seem inclined to open them for anything. I guided her through the door. Once we were clear of the wreckage, I shifted around behind her. My hands wrapped around her, so when I kicked my fins, they didn't hit her.

We glided under the flames, angling toward the surface. As I looked up, I thought we'd made it past the fire, and we continued up.

Sunlight offered a disparate environment from the dark cabin. The woman thrashed a bit as we came up.

My regulator popped out of my mouth as I tried to soothe her. "Calm down. I still have you."

She relaxed a bit, but her body was still taut with fear. *Beth* was about 50 feet away from where we surfaced.

"I'm going to roll on my back," I told her. "Use me like a float."

She obeyed, pulling up on my inflated BCD as I kicked backwards toward the dinghy.

In order to get into *Beth* from deep water, I made a contraption that strapped across the boat and came up under the hull. When my weight pressed down on the rope ladder, the opposite side of the boat took an equal amount of pressure. That way, the dinghy didn't flip over on me.

The woman put her foot on the first rung of the ladder, and I used my hand against her butt to shove her up into the boat. I knew it was inappropriate given the circumstances, but I mentally admired the firm muscles on her backside.

"The crew!" she exclaimed.

"I didn't see them," I told her. "How many were there?"

She panted. "Three. Two pilots and an attendant."

I glanced back at the sinking plane.

"If I don't come back," I explained, "take the dinghy to that sailboat over there."

She followed the direction of my finger to the shape of *Carina* in the distance. Before she acknowledged me, I let the air out of my BCD and swam beneath the flames.

When I reached the entrance to the cabin, I checked the depth—72 feet. I didn't have long. When I entered, I took a few seconds to look around. The first time I swam straight to the back of the plane.

Below me, an opening led to a small cubby. Inverting myself, I pulled my head down for a look. Strapped in a seat against the starboard wall was the attendant, a young woman in her 20s with brown hair that floated at an odd angle to her face. A gash on her temple was probably the result of something striking her during the impact. The injury didn't look life-threatening, but it might have rendered her unconscious, leaving the water to finish her.

I felt the lump in my throat. Dead bodies weren't new to me, but I didn't like them.

She didn't have any identification on her, and searching her body seemed intrusive. There wasn't even any jewelry that could be returned to her family. Maybe it was a company policy. Anything personal was stowed. It made me sadder to think of that for some reason.

I shook the feeling off and moved deeper. The wall between the cabin and the cockpit had buckled. The impact must have rippled through the plane. I pulled the door open to see two men buckled into the seats. The windshield was nothing but a jagged, gaping hole, but the view of the ocean below was surreal.

Both men had name plates on their shirts. I ripped them both off. It was something to take back to the families. Both name tags fit in the front pocket of my BCD.

The black box.

It occurred to me as I was about to turn and head out. If I retrieved that little container of information, the authorities could figure out what happened.

My problem was I did not know what a black box looked like. It seemed like the kind of thing that should have a bold label on it. I assumed that, despite the name, it was neither black nor a box. Probably the closest it would come would be a hard drive of some type.

My face moved closer to the instrument panel, searching for anything.

No luck.

Everything seemed securely attached or torn apart during the impact. No in-between. One entire panel was missing from the left side of the cockpit, while the other had no damage.

As I tried to change direction, the valves on my cylinder caught a tangle of loose wires. The threads wrapped around the knob, catching me in place. I pushed back, trying to come back out the other way.

The wires seemed to get more tangled around my cylinder. The knobs were just an inch out of my reach. If I strained, my fingertips brushed against the wires, but it was too far for me to grab them.

Dammit, I cursed to myself. I'll just cut them loose, I decided.

My hand felt along my calf to unsheathe my dive knife. The knife wasn't there. In my rush to get in the water, I never attached it to my leg. The six-inch blade was sitting on the bottom of *Beth* right now.

Shit. Shit. Shit.

It's just wires, Gordon. Rip them out.

My hand reached back and found the tangle of wires. There was no way to unwind them from the cylinder, but at least I got a grip on them. My hand wrapped them around itself several times before pulling. The cables didn't want to budge. I jerked again. Still nothing.

My knees pulled up against my stomach, and I let the bottom of my feet press against the side of the cockpit. With all my strength, I tried to straighten my legs, pulling against the tendrils that were binding me.

Nothing happened.

I tried again. With what I perceived as more force, I shoved my feet off the side. Several wires snapped, and I flew forward until the remaining ones caught me.

"Damn," I screamed through my regulator.

The cockpit shifted, and the debris twirling around changed direction as the plane upended itself.

My eyes turned up, or at least what I thought was up. The plane must have completely submerged. It was beginning its plummet. The only stop was about 10,000 feet below me.

3

The cockpit rolled, throwing me against the wall. Tethered by the cables holding me, I couldn't escape. The motion seemed slow as the plane's weight rotated around. Something stabbed my leg, and the salt water burned the exposed wound.

My eardrums flexed inside my head as the pressure increased. With a swift motion, my right index finger and thumb squeezed my nose as I blew out some air. The act relieved the pressure before my eardrums burst.

My attention turned to the stabbing sensation in my thigh. A corner of one panel must have been bent back during the initial impact. Now it skewered the back of my leg, about four inches above my knee. I pushed up off the panel. The metal shard pulled out of the muscle. Red streams streaked from the cut like a thin plume of smoke. Thankfully, it didn't hit the artery. Just a small vein. It wouldn't kill me.

Of course, the rapid drop to the ocean floor would take care of that.

My hand swept back to grab my depth gauge. It was a waste of time that should be used attempting to get out, but my survival instinct wanted to know how bad my situation was. The needle moved steadily up, passing 90.

It was bad. As fast as that needle climbed, things progressed from bad to worse by each second.

Come on, Chase.

After getting back up against the wall, my feet pushed against the side of the cockpit, trying to free myself from the knot of cables wrapped around the cylinder.

Nothing budged. The wires tightened, preventing me from moving forward.

I cursed through my regulator. When I entered the plane, the depth didn't require deco, or decompression. The human body isn't designed to be under the sea, and even with the correct gear, the diver has to be wary of nitrogen build up in the blood. The deeper the dive, the quicker the body absorbs the nitrogen. Failure to maintain a low nitrogen absorption could cause nitrogen narcosis, which is a nasty way to die.

If the diver stays at deep depths for too long, they have to make measured stops during the ascent to prevent decompression sickness, or the bends. The body will attempt to expel the gas as the water pressure lessens, only if the rise happens too fast, the nitrogen basically bubbles up in the bloodstream. It can cause all sorts of problems, including burst blood vessels and embolisms. An equally nasty way to die.

I didn't want to be forced to choose between manners of death.

The pressure in my head increased again. Another blast of air cleared my ears. It was a temporary respite as I fell deeper.

As the plane plummeted toward the ocean depth, I was acutely aware of my predicament. My deepest dive ever reached 185 feet, but I was breathing a nitrox mix of air designed for deep water diving. We were on a training mission about 400 miles north of here. Even if I'd run into trouble on that dive, there was a rescue team, a medical center, and a decompression chamber ready to save me. With only a regular tank of air strapped to my back, it limited me to 130 feet without some serious decompression stops on the way up.

There was no one on the surface ready to come save me. I was all alone. If I died, no one would know until the woman I saved got to shore.

Of course, if she didn't know how to change out a fuel pump, she might be stuck out here for a long time too.

Worse than worrying about making deco stops was the fact that at some point going down, the depth would kill me outright. Not from being crushed. The ocean isn't deep enough to create the amount of pressure to pulverize bones, but it will do a good number on muscle and tissue. I wouldn't know it because the nitrogen narcosis would overtake me first.

A brief thought crossed my mind. This was all the fault of that damn fuel pump. I could have been cruising along and never seen the jet dive into the ocean.

My knees bent, and I heaved against the wall again. I had no intention of being left in a watery grave.

Nothing moved.

Dammit.

I didn't have time to try anything else. In seconds, the plane would hit a depth I'd never escape. My hand fumbled as I unlatched the buckle on my BCD and slipped it off my shoulders. It seemed like my only choice. Once free, I could turn to see the cylinder's knobs.

It was insane, but that action paid off. My hands found the electrical cables snaking out of the shattered console. The wire had wrapped three or four times around the knob as if it tied me up intentionally. The crisscrossing lines held better than my hitch knots at the dock. My fingers worked with haste to untangle the wires as fast as I could move.

A shiver ran through my body. The temperature of the water was dropping, and the pressure on my ears intensified. I cleared them multiple times as I worked the wire.

As soon as the last strand came free, I kicked my feet toward the cockpit door. As the plane was still tumbling, I had no way of knowing which direction was up. The aircraft pitched around and putting the BCD back on would only take away precious seconds.

My depth gauge said 140 feet. Keeping the BCD pressed against me, I struggled past the flight attendant's body to the main cabin. My eyes focused on the door, trying not to offer the attendant any sympathetic glances. Right now, my only goal needed to be to escape or else she and I would have an eternity together.

Hurry up, Chase,

The door was closed, having swung shut as the plane tumbled in its descent. The water pressure was pinning it closed. I needed more than my strength to open it.

The next couple of seconds provided the opportunity I needed. My shoulder pressed against it as that side of the plane rotated down. Gravity still works underwater, and the door swung open.

I kicked out and curled into a ball with the BCD in my arms. The exterior of the plane hit my body. The blow was harder than I expected, and I spun away from the jet. It felt like I was a pinball spiraling across open water. After several rolls, I slowed enough to straighten myself, but between the rapid exit and continued drop, I was utterly disoriented. I needed to go up, but I was certain I was still sinking.

My thumb pressed the button to inflate the BCD. While I couldn't ascend too fast, I needed to stop my drop. It felt like nothing was happening. With my left arm wrapped around the BCD, my right uncinched the belt at my waist, holding the extra 20 pounds of lead weight. The belt slid through the buckle and dropped below me.

At least I was sure which way was up.

My fins began pedaling slowly toward the surface as I grabbed the depth gauge. 176 feet.

After hitting those depths, I needed to make a slow ascent—no more than 30 feet per minute. Once I reached safer levels, I needed to make a decompression stop.

The whistle of air filling the BCD and the bubbles as I exhaled were the only thing I could hear in the abyss. I scolded myself for not judging the direction the bubbles were going.

It wasn't quite dark, but everything seemed dim. The sunlight was still visible, but it was like seeing it through a shade.

After a minute, I reached 150 feet. My grip on the BCD was like a vice. The last thing I needed was to lose my grip on it. The inflatable vest would shoot up without my weight, leaving me struggling with deciding between a rapid free diving ascent coupled with the bends or drowning. Given how far I was from medical treatment, both would be a death sentence.

I paused long enough to slip my arms back into the BCD. Each arm wound through the hole while the other clung to the vest.

Once I secured the BCD around me again, I breathed a little easier. Until I checked my air levels. When I entered the water the first time, I had 1,200 p.s.i., which would usually last me just over an hour in ideal circumstances where my depth was less than 100 feet, and I was enjoying a leisurely dive.

However, after sharing air with the woman and some exerted breathing during my escape from the cockpit, I was down to 400 p.s.i. My safety net for returning to the surface is about 500. That's enough to ensure if something goes wrong, I have a little air to fill my BCD and breathe for several more minutes.

I hadn't timed myself in the plane, but I estimated I spent at least five minutes at 170 feet. Since the plane was dropping, I figured it was much less, but better safe than sorry. My dive computer attached to my depth gauge does all the calculations for decompression stops. Mine suggested a deco stop at 60 feet. That was 90 feet above me, which would require three minutes to reach safely.

Breathe slowly, Chase.

Without adding air to the BCD, I kicked slowly up, allowing my natural buoyancy to lift me. It was a balance to reduce my exertion to conserve air and still cover the distance in the required time frame.

When I reached 60 feet, I checked my air consumption. 350 p.s.i. I hovered there for three minutes. My brain worked to regulate my breathing to conserve every bit.

After three minutes, I rechecked my air. 320 p.s.i. I groaned. My breathing was always heavy, no matter how slow I tried to take it.

My feet pedaled me toward the surface. At 30 feet, I stopped for another three minutes. According to most dive instructors, I was safe after the first stop. However, I didn't time my descent, and it might have been faster than it should have been. Again, better safe than sorry. I'd seen what happens to divers that get the bends. I've only ever had a very mild case, resulting in a splitting headache. The idea of having worse happen didn't appeal to me.

After my three minutes were up, I still had over 200 p.s.i. in the cylinder. Enough to fill my BCD and take a slow, easy ascent.

My eyes squinted as the sun blinded me when I popped out of the water. A quick spin allowed me to orient myself. *Beth* was almost 200 yards away. The flames from the wreckage appeared to have all been extinguished.

I rolled onto my back and kicked toward the dinghy. Now that I was breathing fresh air, I let my mind roll the last few minutes around. Three people were buried beneath me. An hour ago, they were all just doing their jobs. Completely unaware of what was coming.

I'm not really a praying person. Which isn't to say I'm not spiritual. There has to be a higher power; I'm just not sure how involved He gets.

Nonetheless, I prayed those three found a better world where they went.

I realized my legs were tiring as I neared the tender. My mask slipped over my head, and I dropped it into the boat.

The woman didn't make a sound.

"You okay?" I asked.

Silence.

I lifted up on my fins to peer over the gunwale. The blond survivor was curled in a fetal position. She was asleep. The crash of adrenaline will do that. She was near death, fighting for survival, and now the fear had passed. Her body gave out.

She'd sleep for a while. Hopefully, I could get her up long enough to board *Carina*.

Within a minute, I had hoisted my gear into *Beth*, and we were heading back to *Carina*.

4

The engine purred as *Carina* sliced through the glassy water. Once I helped the woman on board, she curled up in the rear cabin without hardly a word. She mumbled something when I directed her down the companionway, but it was gibberish from someone who had barely gotten out of REM sleep.

Her slumber was solid enough that my knocking around the engine room, just a few feet from her berth, didn't stir her. After getting *Beth* stowed along with my gear, I dropped onto the cockpit cushion as exhaustion took over. My eyes closed for about 30 minutes before my stomach reminded me it remained empty.

The Mahi seemed too much effort after the rescue, and I settled for some cheese and crackers. Another hour tinkering around the engine room netted a fully functional Perkins engine.

When I turned the key, *Carina* cranked up without a hiccup. A sigh of relief escaped my lips as I slumped back in the cockpit.

The only question at that point was where to go. Belize was still a day or two away. Maybe three if the wind never picked up.

That might be too long out of communication. My mind drew back to those three crew members that rested at the bottom of the sea. The jet would be reported as missing, and a search might take place. During those hours, the families would be in turmoil, wondering what happened to their loved ones.

The news I offered wouldn't console anyone, but at least the answers might bring closure. The grieving won't start until all hope is extinguished.

When I pulled up my location on the chart plotter, the closest port was just over a hundred miles southeast. The Swan Islands.

I knew little about them. Based on a recent cruising guide I picked up for the western Gulf of Mexico, the Swan Islands consisted of two small chunks of land just enough out of the way to avoid being on most people's list. The only thing on them was a Honduran Naval Post. It might not have any amenities, but hopefully, the post would have a satellite phone or some means to reach the mainland.

With *Carina* pointed toward the southeast, I rested on the cockpit, allowing the autopilot to maintain our heading. The wind remained abated, leaving the main sail luffing from the mast. I kept the boom tight so that it wouldn't make wild swings from port to starboard. If a breeze came along, it took me opening one cam cleat to release the sheet, letting the sail catch the gust and swing the boom either way.

So far, there was no threat of wind. The water remained slick, and the only waves were large, rounded ones that never crested but just kept the boat on a gentle roll. While we trudged along, I tossed two lines off the stern with bait attached. With another mouth to feed, I might need another Mahi-mahi or, if I was extremely lucky, a yellowfin tuna.

Today could have been a perfectly relaxing day if I hadn't been face to face with three corpses and nearly dragged to the ocean floor.

When we were in Afghanistan or Iraq, the hours following a mission were surreal. In a fire-fight or any combat, time has this unusual ability to slow to a crawl. Five minutes will seem like an hour. Hours become days. Even in retrospect, the event never seems to correct that perspective.

I was inside the plane for less than 10 minutes. If I include the first dive, it might have been 15. Normally, the timer in my head is clicking off the seconds. Once the plane started its dive, the clock stopped working.

Those minutes dragged into forever.

Now, I'm staring across the vast blue waters, pondering my mortality. Today wasn't my first encounter with it. I certainly doubted it would be my last. However, if coming face-to-face with the Reaper doesn't give one pause to consider and recollect, then it might be the time has come. I'm not ready to die yet, but it's never been something to fear.

Of course, as Marines, the possibility wasn't allowed. Marines don't give up, certainly not to something as trivial as Death.

Nonetheless, it occurred to me that had those moments been my last, the end would be fitting. Since leaving my home for Parris Island, I didn't have a home except *Carina*. She seemed more like home when she was free of the dock.

Still, I wasn't ready just yet.

Below deck, a noise emanated through the companion-way doors. My visitor sounded like she had awakened.

Several seconds later, the teak double doors swung open. Her face appeared in the crack. For the first time, I got a good look at her. Her eyes were no longer bloodshot from the tears, but instead, the pale blue irises shone out, reminding me of the shallow, sandy waters around the Bahamas.

"Hello," I greeted her.

"Uh...hello," she responded.

"How are you feeling?"

She blinked a couple of times, as if trying to understand what she was looking at. Finally, she mustered, "I'm tired."

I nodded. "I'm Chase, by the way. Chase Gordon."

"Allie," she told me. "Tremblay."

"Nice to meet you, Allie Tremblay," I offered.

"Uh, is there a bathroom?" she asked.

"Of course," I answered, as I stood up. "Let me show you."

Allie stepped back to give me room to climb down the companionway stairs. I squeezed past her to walk forward.

"The head is through those doors," I explained, pointing to an accordion-style door. "It's not like a regular toilet. There's a switch that you move to unlock it after you've done your business. Then, pump the handle until all the water has flushed. Once you're done, flip the switch back to lock it."

She nodded like everyone does before they use the marine toilet. Three out of five times, the person needs to ask for help. The confinements brought on by being on a boat with someone tend to remove the awkward ignorance about bodily functions. Everyone is too close to pretend it doesn't happen.

"I'll be up top, if you need me," I informed her.

"Thank you," she uttered softly.

On my way on deck, I pulled a bottled water from the refrigerator and set it on the counter for her. I doubted she'd drank anything in hours. With my bottle in my hand, I returned to the cockpit.

The label had faded over time. Since trash can be a concern on a 40-foot boat, I try to conserve as much as I can. All my water bottles are reused. I clean and rinse them before refilling them with fresh purified water. I figure it's my compromise between the convenience and luxury of cold water versus the bane of plastic. Once I reach a port where recycling is common, I'll trade out the old bottles for a new pack.

On the helm, the paperback I'd been reading before the fuel pump crapped out on me, waited for me to pick the story back up. I thumbed through the pages, but my mind wasn't ready to dive into it at the moment. I tossed the worn book back on top of the wheel and leaned back.

The doors opened again, and Allie reappeared.

"Is this water for me?" she asked.

"Yeah," I responded. "There's food in there too if you want anything."

She hoisted the water, saying, "I'll start with this, if that's okay."

I nodded. "Want to come up?"

Her eyes darted around. At first, I thought she was scoping out the cockpit, but after a second, it was obvious she was looking out over the ocean. Many people question what it's like to be out of sight of land. Does it scare me? What if something goes wrong? The idea can be nerve-wracking.

I couldn't fathom how Allie felt. She left wherever she was, never planning to be stuck in the middle of the ocean.

She climbed the steps carefully and sat on the cockpit bench.

"You okay?" I asked.

She nodded nervously, which might have been easier than lying.

"Were you just out here?" Curiosity laced her tone.

"Yeah," I confirmed. "Right place, wrong time."

"Not for me, I guess," she remarked.

Her tone was soft, but firm. I imagined in a different circumstance she would come across stronger.

"I'm sorry about your crew," I commented. There wasn't much I could say. No point in giving her the details unless she wanted them.

"I didn't really know them," she told me. "The flight attendant said her name was Carly."

"Was it your plane?" I asked.

She made a half nod, half shake with her head as if to say "kind of."

"It was a company plane," she explained. "Really, like a rental, I guess."

I nodded. Company plane. She was the only passenger. That made her important in the company.

"Your company?"

"More like my father's company," she replied. "Or, at least, it was."

Did that mean her father was dead? Was he on the plane too?

Allie must have seen the questions on my face. She told me, "He died in a car accident in Panama a week ago. I flew down to collect some personal things from his office and bring his remains home."

Her mouth frowned at the thought.

His remains. He was still on the plane.

"I'm so sorry," I offered.

She shrugged. "He actually wanted to be buried at sea."

My lips pursed. I doubted he was looking for something so unceremonious as crashing into the sea.

"I'm sorry about how I reacted in the plane," she apologized.

"Allie, don't worry," I assured her. "You did nothing wrong. It was an insane moment, and you're entitled to react accordingly."

Tears welled up in her eyes. "I thought I was dead."

My eyes connected with hers as I listened.

"Suddenly, you pop up out of nowhere. It scared the hell out of me."

"I can only imagine," I acknowledged.

"Do you think the crew suffered?" she asked.

I shook my head. "I think the crash itself killed them. Since you were in the back of the plane, you avoided the initial impact."

"I should have tried to get out of there," she muttered.

There was something she wasn't talking about yet. It was obvious from the way her eyes kept looking out across the sea and then cutting down to her hands. Allie was terrified of the water. Maybe she never learned to swim or something traumatic branded that fear in her. Whatever triggered that fear left her petrified in the back row of the jet while it sank in the sea.

Not that it would have mattered. If she had been able to get out, and even if she'd found the life raft, the plane went down hundreds of miles from shore. Once the plane was overdue, a search might begin, but the area would be thousands of square miles of open ocean. The odds of being rescued were almost zero.

Unless one factors in a boat bum with a bad fuel pump and no wind. But I guess those kinds of things are beyond the predictability. I wondered what odds Las Vegas would place on that happening.

"You did what you needed to do," I promised her. "Sometimes survival is just holding on for another minute."

"What are you doing out here?" she asked incredulously.

I took a sip of water before answering, "I was on my way to Belize."

"Why?"

"I wanted to dive the Big Blue Hole," I told her.

She looked confused.

"Off the coast of Belize is a big hole in the ocean. It's surrounded by reefs and just drops off to about 125 feet. I've never been to Belize, and diving the reefs there have been on my bucket list."

She nodded. "Do you live on your boat?"

"Yeah, it's home. I used to be in the Marine Corps, but since I got back into civilian life, I've lived on *Carina*."

"Your boat's name is *Carina*?"

"She's named after a dog I had when I was younger," I explained. "Where are you from, Allie?"

She glanced up, staring off at the afternoon sun. "Toronto."

"Canada, huh?"

She nodded. "It was just my dad and me," she told me. "Now, I guess, it's just me."

"No other family?"

"I have a sister, Sara. She's been in a coma for the last ten months. The doctors don't think she'll ever recover."

"I'm so sorry," I offered.

She shrugged again, as if this was just the way life was.

"Her husband, Steven, is around. He works...worked for Daddy."

"What kind of business is it?"

"Ever hear of Banyan Freight?" she questioned.

My eyebrow lifted. It was hard to float anywhere on the ocean and not hear about Banyan Freight. Their container ships passed through every port in the world. While I didn't see a lot of their ships in the Bahamas, they littered the Miami area, delivering goods from all over the world to the United States.

"I've heard of them. That's your company?"

"It is now," she acknowledged.

I held my tongue, but the word "wow" almost slipped out. Banyan Freight had to be worth billions. Here I was entertaining an heiress with bottles of refilled water.

As I was about to ask Allie about her sister, one of the lines I'd tossed off the stern went taut. I twisted around to reel it in. A greenish blob splashed off the back of the boat. Another Mahi.

"What's that?" Allie asked.

"Dinner," I remarked as I turned to look at her. "That is, if you like seafood."

She nodded.

Five minutes later, a medium-sized Mahi was flopping around the sole of the cockpit.

"I have to kill it," I warned her. "If that makes you squeamish."

She frowned. "I've hunted every year since I was 9 years old."

Without another word, I used a knife to finish the fish. After several minutes, I sliced the fish into steaks and fired up the grill.

5

The sunrise splayed red across the horizon. *Carina* sloshed through the waves that had grown overnight. The breeze finally kicked up around three in the morning. With the red sky flaming over the sea, I knew the changes in weather must be the harbinger of a storm. Every sailor knew the rhyme: *Red sky at night, sailor's delight. Red sky in morning, sailor take warning.* A storm was coming.

Bad weather is just a part of life at sea. While blue skies and light breezes create a perfect day, life has to deal us lemons now and then. Sailing through a storm is never fun. It takes constant concentration, a steady hand at the helm, and a good amount of cursing.

This storm was still hours away. In fact, I expect it would come late this evening. While I'm out of sight of land, the only weather forecasts I can get come over the single side-band radio or SSB. The SSB allows me to get weather updates from a few sources, however most focus on the heavier trafficked waters. Sometimes, I relied on my instinct. Based on my past performance, I get about a 60 percent accuracy rating. Of course, I am the one giving out those ratings, so take it as you will.

Ahead, a small grayish mound rose out of the water. One of the Swan Islands had come into view. As long as the Honduran military did not turn us away, we should be safely harbored for the storm tonight.

Allie was sleeping below. Given her obvious fear and lingering shock, it didn't seem prudent to ask her to keep watch. I napped a little during the night, but overall, I maintained a vigilant watch. Once the wind picked up, I raised the jib and rode along without the motor.

The local time was just after six. Someone should be up on the island. I lifted the radio and transmitted, "Swan Island, this is the *Sailing Vessel Carina*, come in."

The response was silence. I repeated my call.

The receiver squawked and an accented voice responded in rapid Spanish. My high school Spanish was less than desirable, and I wasn't able to understand any of what he said.

"*Quiero anclar, por favor,*" I attempted, hoping the man on the other end of the radio understood the phrase, "I want to anchor, please."

"*Sí. Ve al lado norte de la isla.*"

I understood "yes," "north," and "island."

"*Gracias,*" I responded over the radio.

The doors opened, and Allie climbed up on deck. Before she went to bed, I showed her where the life vests were located, even pulling one out so that she had easy access to it. I wanted her to feel comfortable and relax a little, but I knew that there was little chance of that.

"Were you up all night?" she asked.

"I dozed a bit, but mostly."

"How do you do that?"

I shrugged. "It's part of cruising. There's an autopilot, so I don't have to keep a close watch. Also, the radar will let me know if something comes within range."

She shook her head. "I think I'd be too deep asleep."

"I learned to sleep light and quick in the Corps. It's a vital rule–sleep when you can."

"I guess," she acknowledged as she looked across the water. "Is that land?"

"The Swan Islands," I confirmed. "We should be able to get a message out about your plane."

"Do you think they know we crashed yet?" she wondered.

"I imagine you were due back sometime last night. The authorities at least are concerned because you are overdue and incommunicado."

She was quiet for a minute.

"Did your father live in Panama?" I asked after some time.

"No, but we have an office there. He spent a lot of time down there. Well, he and Steven both."

"What does your brother-in-law do for the company?"

"He's Vice President of Logistics."

"Ah," I commented.

She ignored my obvious ignorance. "How long before we get there?"

"With the wind building up, I'd say less than an hour."

Relief passed over her face. Allie was ready for some solid ground.

As my hull speed increased to about 12 knots, I stood and started keeping a more vigilant watch. The chart plotter highlighted the waters around the island with lines showing the depth. As we neared the land, the sea shallowed to 12 to 15 feet around them.

"I never understood how an island can just pop up in the middle of the ocean," Allie commented.

"I think these are technically mountaintops. There's a range of mountains that run along the ocean floor. These just happen to be the tallest."

"Really?" Her head popped up at that realization. "It's weird to think about a mountain range underwater. Imagine what it would look like."

A smile grew across my face. "Oh, the thought has crossed my mind. There is so much to explore down there. I know there are so many companies racing to get to space, but I'd love to explore the ocean floor myself. It must be cool to take a sub down through a canyon so deep that no one can survive there. What might be down there that no one has ever seen?"

She nodded.

I noticed a dark area ahead of us. My chart plotter showed what was probably a shallow reef. The bottom was rising fast now, and I sprung over to retract the jib. The SOG meter which measures the speed over ground showed a sudden drop from 12 knots to 7 as *Carina* propelled forward only under the main-sail.

"I don't suppose you speak Spanish?" I asked.

"I'm not quite fluent but I'm passable."

"Good," I remarked. "Mine is abysmal. We might need it."

"Shouldn't a world traveler, such as yourself, be able to speak the language of the places you visit."

"I'm passable in Pashto," I pointed out.

Her brow furrowed.

"They speak it in Afghanistan."

"Oh," she responded. "Doesn't help much here."

"I'm planning to learn," I informed her. "I just haven't yet."

The waters slowly morphed colors, changing from the deep blue to a pale tone. The waters were crystal clear, and as we coursed through 30 feet of water, the rocks and coral heads beneath us were easily visible.

Twenty minutes later, I released the cleat securing the main halyard and lowered the anchor. Once the anchor set securely in the sand, I climbed on top of the cabin and flaked the main sail. When the cam cleat releases the main halyard, gravity brings the sail down, where it gathers in a clump. I try to straighten the mess and fold it so that it remains neat and tidy. With a couple of strands of fabric, I secure the sail, so it rests on the boom.

We floated in 12 feet of water about 50 yards from a sandy beach. Three men trudged from the tree line toward the water, where they stood watching me secure *Carina*.

"Is this as close as we get?" Allie asked.

"'Fraid so. The keel goes down seven and a half feet. I don't want to mire it in the sand, so we'll take the dinghy to shore."

Her face contorted for a split second before she mustered control. "Okay," she responded warily.

I climbed below deck and returned with a single bottle of Jack Daniels Tennessee Whiskey.

"What's that for?" she asked.

"Diplomatic relations," I explained. "Miss Manners says one should never show up without a gift for the host."

Allie stared at me, and I waved her off.

After lowering *Beth* into the water, I handed the life vest to Allie. "Why don't you put this on?" I encouraged.

Without a word, she obeyed. Once she secured the vest around her torso, I helped her into the tender. As close as we were, I would normally just grab the oars and row myself to shore. It's excellent exercise and only takes a few extra minutes. Today, I wanted to get the ride over as quickly as possible for Allie, so I pulled the cord and started the little motor.

Half a minute later, I killed the engine and let the hulls plow into the sand. My feet splashed into the surf, and I grabbed the painter attached to the bow, dragging the dinghy up onto the beach.

Two of the men rushed over to help Allie out of the boat as the third, a lanky man approached me.

"I'm Captain Rojas," he introduced.

"Chase Gordon," I responded, extending my hand in greeting.

As he took my hand, he asked, "What brings you to our island?"

I gestured toward Allie. "This is Allie Tremblay. I rescued her from a downed plane yesterday about 200 kilometers northwest of here. You were the closest place to land, and I'm hoping she can call and alert the authorities."

Rojas let his face twist with concern. "Were others aboard?"

"Three crew," I told him. "They were killed during the crash."

"Terrible news," he consoled as the two men escorted Allie over.

None of the men wore uniforms. A post like this was likely very casual. No brass is popping in unannounced to inspect.

"Captain Rojas, I brought a gift." My hand came up, offering the bottle of whiskey.

The man studied the bottle and smiled. The other two men shared in his mirth.

"Come Mr. Gordon. Make yourself at home."

"We appreciate your hospitality," I remarked. "Do you have a phone or radio?"

"Of course, Manuel will show you to the satellite phone," he told Allie before sputtering a command in Spanish to Manuel.

"Thank you, Captain."

The captain stared at the tattoo peeking out from under my sleeve. "Were you in the military?" he questioned.

"Marine Corps," I answered.

"Wonderful, a fellow soldier-in-arms," he announced. "Come, let me show you our tiny base."

The base comprised two barracks, a mess hall, the captain's quarters, and a recreational area. The complement of soldiers consisted of eight men. According to the captain, they worked a six-month rotation before being transferred back to the mainland.

Between the two barracks, the men had built a fire pit with a spit for roasting meats. They strung several hammocks between palm trees. The entire island almost resembled a tropical summer camp.

"I have a nice size Mahi I caught yesterday," I told the captain. "Would your men enjoy it?"

The officer grinned. "My men love an opportunity to eat and drink. Tonight, we can feast on it. We have some fresh fruit as well. The men stationed here over the years have taken to cultivating several pineapple and mango trees."

"Sounds delicious," I commented.

Rojas lifted the bottle of Jack Daniels and stated, "We will drink and toast to those we lost."

I nodded. The man had an infectious personality, and he was hard to not like.

Manuel and Allie marched toward us from the mess hall where the phone was.

"Any luck?" I asked.

"I talked to Bryan White. He's the Operational Director. The plane was considered missing yesterday, and a search was going to start this morning. He promised to pass along the news to the crews' families."

"Good news," the captain noted.

"He's arranging for someone to pick me up tomorrow. The next day at the latest. He said it might take a few days since we are pretty far off the grid."

"You are welcome to stay here as long as you require, Ms. Tremblay," the captain offered.

"Thank you."

"In fact, we have plenty of extra bunks for you to sleep in."

I smiled, and my eyes cut to Manuel. There was probably not a bit of danger in that for Allie, but these men didn't have any women around for six months. Caution would be better, I decided.

"We wouldn't want to impose," I responded. "We have plenty of room on *Carina* to sleep. However, I'm sure we are all looking forward to dinner this evening."

6

The empty bottle of Jack Daniels rested on its side. A second bottle, once full of Honduran guaro, sat beside the square bottle. The men on Swan Island could drink. Boy, could they drink.

I kept up with them through the entire bottle of Jack, but after three shots of the guaro, I pulled back. The sweet, rotgut liquor is a staple in Central America. The closest I could associate it with was rum, but the alcohol content of guaro was low. Unfortunately, it was simply too sweet, and I grew tired of it.

But the Honduran Navy continued through two more bottles. I'd have developed diabetes before I could catch a buzz off that.

The Hondurans went all out for dinner, bringing out buckets of crab and lobster they caught in the reefs off-shore. Captain Rojas had one of his men, Ortiz, take some of the Mahi I brought ashore to make a ceviche with fresh lime. They grilled the rest of the Mahi on hot stones along with fresh tortillas.

Ortiz seemed to be the cook for the group. The fish was nearly perfect, flaky, and moist. The crab and lobster were boiled with some type of potato.

Allie became the center of attention. She was fluent enough to converse with each of them in Spanish, and the result was obvious. Every man vied for her attention. She was the only girl at the dance.

"You don't care for the guaro?" the captain asked as he took a seat next to me. The fire was still burning, but most of the wood had reduced to embers.

"No, it's good. Too sweet for me to drink it all night."

"I would agree," he replied. "I prefer the Jack Daniels."

The corners of my mouth lifted. "I have another bottle on the boat," I suggested.

Rojas grinned. "No, I think I should remain clear-headed."

He eyed the most recent man to engage Allie in conversation. He struck me as a wizened commander. How did he get a post as isolated as this?

"How long is your tour here?" I asked.

"Six more weeks," he responded. "Although, I imagine I will remain on the island."

I nodded. The questions in my head were too personal to ask. That left me to speculate, which does no one any good.

"It is getting late," he surmised. "I'll be calling the evening to an end within a few minutes. We still have duties to perform."

"Understood, Captain. I appreciate the hospitality."

He beamed. "It's our pleasure. There are few visitors to our island."

I picked up the glass, half full of guaro, and lifted it to him. "To visiting again. Under less tragic circumstances," I offered.

He clinked his glass against mine before we both drained the liquor from them.

After a few minutes of shared silence, the captain rose to his feet, announcing something in Spanish. The translation must have been an order that the evening must end. The Honduran men began cleaning the area, gathering trash and leftover food. Allie took the opportunity to pull away from the last man still talking to her as he got to his feet. With some grace, she excused herself and walked in my direction.

"Weren't you the hit of the ball?" I remarked.

Even in the remaining firelight, I could see her face flush. She commented, "They were all very sweet. The last one just wanted to tell me all about his daughter."

"Must get lonely out here," I thought aloud.

"You don't have much room to talk," she pointed out.

I shrugged. "You ready to go back to the boat?"

She didn't answer immediately, but her entire body seemed to squirm, as if everything was just uncomfortable.

"I guess we need to," she remarked after a second.

"Or" I suggested, "we get a couple of hammocks and find a couple of nice cozy palm trees on a beach."

Her face brightened. Anything to keep her on dry land was worth pursuing.

"That would be nice," she admitted. "We can hear the surf."

"Come on," I urged her, taking her by the hand. "Let's see if we can find a spot."

We walked along the shoreline. Despite her fear of water, Allie had no qualms about wading barefoot through the surf as it lapped up on the sand. Crabs scampered from above the waterline toward the foamy sea as we approached.

"It was a nice evening," Allie noted. "The food was amazing."

"Yeah," I replied. "Ortiz really knows his way around a hot rock."

"He told me his father owned a restaurant in his town. That's where he learned to cook."

Ahead of us, the island curved north. We'd walked a little over a quarter of a mile to the eastern end of the island. A hundred feet from the shore, six trees grew in a cluster together.

"How about there?" I asked.

She took several seconds to survey the area. "This seems perfect."

"I'll run back to the boat and grab a couple of hammocks and a blanket," I told her. Chill bumps from the ocean breeze covered her bare arms. "Just wait here. It won't take me long."

Within thirty minutes, I felt the sand shift under *Beth's* hull as I beached the dinghy a few feet from Allie. She was resting on the beach with her knees pulled up against her chest as she stared across the black water.

The wet sand squished through the openings of my sandals as I splashed into the surf. The cool foam washed up my legs. With the breeze coming from the east, the beach was almost chilly in the night air. I pulled two hammocks along with a couple of blankets to shield the wind out of a waterproof bag hooked on Beth's gunwale. A large blue tarp wrapped tightly with six bungee cords remained in the boat. If the morning sky was any indication, we had some rain coming through. While I don't mind a little water, soaking wet is a difficult way to sleep. At the first sign of rain, I could create a makeshift shelter to keep us mostly dry. I doubted Allie would find much rest if it stormed, but at least she didn't have to get back on the boat.

I dropped onto the sand next to her. Her face was soft, but her eyes seemed lost on the horizon.

"It seems so surreal," she commented.

"Yeah," I agreed. She wasn't specific, but I felt those same feelings.

"It was yesterday. I should be dead." Her words and thoughts meandered like a young child slowly traipsing down a street. Each syllable she uttered was trying to understand what the toddler saw. But, I realized, this wasn't the wonderment of discovery. Allie wanted understanding.

"Tonight, I'm partying around a bonfire," she continued. "As if three people didn't die. Or like I'm not supposed to be dead."

"Allie," I tried to say.

"No, Chase," she interrupted. "What if it's too surreal? Or not real at all?"

My hand reached over to touch her arm. She didn't want any platitudes. No suggestions or refutes. I knew those feelings. A cross between survival guilt and relief.

"Do you remember that story?" she asked. "'The Incident at the Owl Bridge' or something like that. I don't remember the name."

"Yeah, I read it in high school."

"What was it called?" she asked.

My head shook. "I'm not sure. I think it was 'Occurrence' not incident."

"Could be," she acknowledged. "They hung a man on a bridge."

I nodded. "Right. But the rope breaks and he falls into the river."

Allie added, "He escapes and runs all the way home. Only when he gets there, or maybe, he's almost there when he realizes the whole thing was in his head. He ends up dying on the bridge as the rope snaps."

I squeezed her arm to reassure her.

"What if my rope hasn't snapped yet?" she pondered.

"Listen, Allie. I know what you are thinking. I've been there. Not a plane crash, but a fire fight when I was stationed in Afghanistan. Five of us entered a building. We weren't even expecting resistance. It was a routine mission. Hell, we'd been in that building to see one of the Afghan guides several times. This time, though, the Taliban was waiting for us. They rigged the building with explosives. Between the bombs and gunfire, only two of us walked out."

She studied me as I told her.

"For weeks after, I wondered how I got out. Why did I get out? Why not the others?"

"Did you find an answer?" she asked.

I shrugged. "Not really. But there were more battles, more death, more everything, and those thoughts still lingered. Less each time, perhaps. But they were still there."

"It doesn't answer much," she pointed out.

"No, it doesn't. I guess I realized it wasn't my time yet. Just like it wasn't your time yesterday."

"I just keep seeing the water coming after me. I'm afraid to close my eyes to sleep."

"The dreams will come," I pointed out. "Just like the sleep will. Remember, it's perfectly acceptable to be alive."

Allie's chin drooped a little. "It happened before too."

"You almost drowned?" I asked.

"Yeah, how did you guess?"

"I think the pale green color your face turns every time you think about being on or in the water was the giveaway."

Allie chuckled. "I'm petrified of it. I'll stick to showers. Even swimming pools make me queasy."

"What happened?"

"I was six years old, and Dad took all four of us to raft the Nith River. Dad was always a rafter, and he wanted to take all of us. The Nith is usually shallow, but during March, the snow melt floods the river. Our raft flipped on one of the rapids. I don't know why, but the current pulled me under. There was a tree submerged down river from the rapids, and I got trapped in the branches. It was horrible. I just remember the darkness all around me. And the cold. It was so cold."

"Dad pulled me out, but not before I had stopped breathing. He performed CPR and resuscitated me. Obviously. But I just remember being rushed to the hospital because of the hypothermia. They said I was under for nearly five minutes."

"That's a long time for a six-year-old," I noted.

"After that, the dreams started. Always the same, I'm underwater trying to get to the surface, only no one else is there. Sometimes it's a tree holding me down. Other times it's a faceless person."

I listened as she continued. "When that water was coming up yesterday, I knew that was it. Even when you popped up, I only saw the tree waiting to take me down."

"It's okay," I assured her. "I'll try to keep you dry while you're with me."

"Good," she responded with a smile. "I prefer it here where I can see the water over there. Like admiring a lion at a zoo. It has its place; I have mine."

"But you're worried about the dreams?"

She nodded. "I haven't had one in years. The last dream was five years ago when my mother died. I hadn't thought about them until now."

"I'm not sure you'll avoid them," I told her. "Everyone has to sleep at some point."

"I know," she admitted, down-hearted.

"You don't have to tonight, though," I advised her. "You can just look at the stars."

"That's always nice." She laid back on the sand, staring up at the swirls of light.

I followed suit. I did not always need a hammock for rest. There have been more than a few occasions when I've slept directly on the beach, watching the stars or clouds dance.

"The stars are so bright here," Allie remarked.

"The view is much better out here than anywhere else."

She fell silent, and I followed the imaginary lines around Taurus. While I sympathized with Allie, I didn't have the same worry about sleep, and in a few minutes, my eyes closed.

The timer in my head told me it was a few minutes after one. The thumping in the distance pulled me awake. Allie was curled up next to me. Despite her fears, she seemed to sleep peacefully.

The sound was getting closer, and I sat up. The breeze had grown into a powerful gust that sprayed the surf up onto us in droplets. On the horizon, lightning lit up the sky, illuminating an ominous wall of clouds. I needed to grab the tarp before that wall hit the island.

The rhythmic beating continued somewhere. My eyes searched the sea for whatever was making the thumping sound. The lights, gliding a few hundred feet above the water's surface, were coming across the ocean from the north. A helicopter.

I stood up and turned for a better view. The chopper looked like a Sikorsky Blackhawk. In the dark, it was hard to distinguish the model. If the lights had been off, the black paint job would have rendered the craft invisible.

My head made some quick calculations. If this was Allie's rescue, it was hours ahead of schedule. Why would they send a Blackhawk? My gut tightened as it hovered over the beach about two miles east of us. Even in the moonless night, I saw the four figures drop out as the chopper descended.

The first gunshot was 60 seconds later.

7

"A llie!" I hissed. "Wake up!"

She stirred a second before sitting up. "What is it?"

More gunfire erupted, followed by shouting. Allie leapt to her feet.

"What's going on?" she muttered.

"I don't know," I admitted. "Come on."

My feet kicked up sand as I broke into a jog. The chopper's turbines were slowing. The pilot was powering it down.

Allie kept up with me, and when I stopped, she nearly ran into me.

"What are you doing?" she questioned.

"Stay here," I ordered.

"What?"

I raised my palm, signaling her to wait. Crouching, I moved into the surf until I was knee deep in the salt water.

The chopper was half a mile away, and I slogged quickly through the knee-deep water.

The blades were turning slowly as the inertia died. A single figure sat in the cockpit, staring toward the barracks. Gunfire continued sporadically. Whoever these guys were, they surprised our hosts. The pilot opened the door, no doubt to let the breeze cool the interior.

He was white and looked very American. My guess was late 40s, but my view wasn't straight on.

The sandals were the kind that strap to my feet. I'd recently tossed every pair of flip-flops I tried. They tore up in the surf or slipped off when I moved around on deck. Even worse, those wretched things offered no traction. It only took one time for my feet to slide off the hull and nearly tear my ACL for me to throw them all away and switch to the hiking sandals.

The other benefit to the sandals was the lack of sound as I crept along the sand behind him. In one fluid motion, I caught the pilot by the shirt and jerked him out of the cockpit. He slammed into the sand. The face-plant stunned him, but I drove my knee into his back.

A .45 Beretta hung in a holster on the belt, holding up his jeans. I whipped it out and pressed it against the back of his head.

"Who are you?" I asked harshly.

"Hey, man, wait," he spat, spewing grains of sand from his face.

"Who the hell are you?" I demanded.

"Name's Royce. David Royce."

"What are you doing here?" I asked.

"Those boys are hitters from the Soria Cartel. I don't know why they wanted to come here, but I fly for them whenever they call."

I glanced up to see Allie approaching slowly.

"The Soria Cartel?" I stammered. "What the hell are they doing here?"

"I don't know. Those guys don't talk to me, and I don't want to talk to them. I just fly when they say fly."

"When did they tell you to fly?"

"I don't know. This morning. About ten or so."

My head looked up at Allie. This morning she called her office. What time was it? I wasn't sure. We dropped anchor around nine. Give us half an hour to dinghy up and talk to Rojas and his men. She called about half-past nine.

My eyes popped back up to Allie before I focused on Royce. "Alright, David, you're going to fly me where I tell you to."

He shook his head, scraping his face through the sand.

"Not a chance," he sputtered. "This is the Soria family. I'm not crossing them for nothing."

"You'd rather cross me?" I asked, pressing the barrel of the Beretta hard against his skull. "That doesn't seem smart, either."

"Look, I don't want to die, but if I take you, they won't just kill me. I have two daughters at home. They'll make examples of my entire family."

Allie pleaded, "Chase, don't."

Frustrated, I pulled the barrel back and cracked Royce on the back of the head. Not enough to cause any major damage, but he'd be out for at least a few minutes.

"We gotta go," I told Allie.

"Where?"

The only way off the island was *Carina*, and Allie would not like that. But every fiber of instinct told me these men were here to finish what the plane crash didn't. I turned and fired two rounds into the controls on the chopper. The only boats I'd seen were two small fishing boats the Hondurans used to patrol the waters. Neither would stand up to the storm approaching. With any luck, the invaders would be stuck until the storm passed.

Behind Allie, the wall of lightning and clouds was almost to the island. We had about ten minutes to pull anchor and run before all hell rained down on the island.

"Come on," I urged.

"Where are we going?"

"We have to get off the island," I explained, taking her hand as I jogged down the beach.

In that instant, she realized what that meant. She'd have to get back on the boat.

"No, no, no," she stuttered. "Can't we just hide?"

"They'd find us. It's not a big island."

"Maybe they will get what they want and leave," she offered.

I shook my head. "I don't think so. My guess is you are what they want."

"Me?" Her eyes widened.

"Let's talk about this once we are safe," I suggested as I continued to move down the beach.

Carina was floating right where we left her. If the storm hit while she was anchored, I felt comfortable with the holding that my 35 pound plow anchor gave me.

Once I pulled the anchor, I had to get away from shore before the wind beached her.

Allie pulled against me. "How are we going to get out there?"

I turned and grabbed her shoulders. "We have to swim."

Her head shook. "I can't swim."

"I'll do all the work. You just have to hold on to me."

A bolt of lightning ripped across the sky as two more gunshots sounded. In the flash of light, I saw the head popping up from the companionway. I dragged Allie to the ground.

"Someone's on the boat," I whispered.

She was close to hyperventilating.

"Stay calm, Allie."

"I'm trying," she sobbed.

There was at least one person on my boat. He needed to be dealt with, but I wasn't sure how I was going to manage that while carrying Allie.

"Listen to me," I demanded. "I don't want you to have to do this, but if you don't, we will die here."

She nodded with fear and tears coming from her eyes.

"Hold on to me with all your might. When we reach the boat, you'll have to hold on to the anchor chain, okay?"

Her face stared up at me. Nothing came out of her mouth, but her lips quivered.

Another flash of lightning lit up the beach.

"We have to go now," I ordered, pulling her onto my back.

Allie obeyed, wrapping her arms around my neck with a vice-like grip. I worried she might choke me if I let her stay on too long, but for now, if it comforted her, then it would work.

On my belly, I crawled through the surf. Allie's face buried into my neck and shoulder. Her whimpers echoed in my ear.

The boat was only 50 yards from the shore. An easy swim, even with a frightened woman clinging to my back. Had I made the approach alone, I'd have remained submerged until I reached the stern. With Allie, I slogged along on the surface, trying to make no noise.

The wind was shaking the boat, and the halyard was clanging against the mast like a dinner bell. I grabbed the anchor chain and pulled Allie around.

"Hold on here," I whispered.

Her eyes remained clenched shut. The tears were mixing with the sea water, but I knew she was still crying. When her hands gripped the chain, her knuckles whitened.

"Don't move," I told her in a hushed voice.

Before she answered, I dipped below the water and swam aft.

Carina has a swim ladder installed on her stern. When I first looked for a boat, I wanted one with a nice swim platform or at least a sugar scoop stern. Somehow, I fell in love with this girl, and I threw all thoughts of easy entry in and out of the sea out. Instead, I designed and built a stowable swim platform I could attach when I'm at an anchorage for a few days. Right now, three bungee cords secured it to the port life lines, making it absolutely no use to me.

The ladder was my only choice. My hand reached up and pulled the rung free. Once I put my weight on the first step, the boat would shift. If the men on board knew anything about boats, it might be a dead giveaway. The Beretta was still in my hand. With a count of three, I grabbed the ladder and hoisted myself up.

The barrel came over the stern rail as my head rose. A dark-skinned man was climbing out of the companion-way. His eyes caught the glint of lightning on the gun before he locked on my face. He pulled what looked like a 9 mm up to fire. He was still halfway in the cabin when the .45 slug knocked him down the steps.

I scampered up to see another man trying to crawl over the first man's body. I pulled the trigger twice, tearing two holes in his chest.

My hand let go of the ladder, and I dropped into the water. There wasn't enough room to hide a third man on board, and Allie might lose it if I didn't get her out of the ocean soon.

"Allie, grab me," I ordered as I came up beside her.

It took me prying her hands off the stainless-steel chain and wrapping them around my neck to get her to let go. When I reached the ladder, I forced her hands to grip the metal rungs. Once she got her foot on the first step, she seemed to regain her confidence as she hurried to get out of the water.

"They're dead," she whispered when I climbed over the stern.

I nodded as I pulled a winch out of the starboard locker. The star gear slipped into the starboard winch. I wound the main sail's halyard around the winch.

"Allie, I need you to crank this. Clockwise. You'll hear the gears click. We have to get the sail up fast."

She nodded and began turning the handle while I ran forward to the anchor. A flash of lightning revealed two men on the beach pointing toward us. I activated the anchor windlass and hurried aft.

The main-sail was halfway up, and the wind filled it, pushing *Carina* toward the shore. I dropped behind the helm as gunfire erupted on the beach. They were shooting at us.

The wheel spun to port as Allie continued to crank the main sail up. Once the rudder pivoted us away from shore, I took hold of the jib sail halyard and started pulling it hand over hand. Normally, I'd use the winch to facilitate this, but Allie was still working the main sail up. As the jib on the bow of the boat unfurled, the wind filled it immediately, nearly ripping the line out of my hand as the entire sail unwound in a split second. My hand stung as the rope sliced through the palm, but I held on to it. *Carina* leapt off the line, jumping to ten knots as she raced away from the island.

"Push that cleat down!" I shouted at Allie, pointing at the black cam cleat forward of the winch she had been working.

She reached up and slapped the cleat down, holding the main sail halyard in place. As I fought to hold on to the jib halyard, I climbed over Allie and wound the line around the winch.

"Grab the wheel!" I yelled back.

Behind us, the storm had caught up. I winched the line until the jib was tight. As I pulled the handle from the winch, the gale caught up. The first raindrops were giant globes of water. The wind rushed behind the rain, blowing at least 40 miles per hour. *Carina* heeled toward starboard at nearly 75 degrees.

"Chase!" Allie screamed. "Help!"

My hand grabbed the wheel, and I adjusted the heading to level the hull. The SOG meter showed us pushing 20 knots, and I didn't like what that might do to the sail. These kinds of gales could shred a sail if I didn't reef it and reduce the sail area.

"Hold this here," I told Allie. "Keep it straight."

When she took the helm again, I released the cleat holding the main sail aloft. The sail lowered as I let the line out until only about a third remained raised. I secured the line before pulling the jib in the same amount.

As I took Allie's place, she asked, "Can't they come after us?"

I shook my head rather than yell above the storm. "Go below," I urged her.

She glanced down at the two corpses, but the appeal of the cabin overcame any trepidation she felt about the dead bodies. The doors closed, and I fought the wheel as the bow plunged through the waves ahead.

The urge to look back was strong, but I couldn't lose my focus. Even if Royce was no longer incapacitated, the chopper hopefully was. If the Soria boys were stupid and fearless, they might venture through this storm after us, but I hoped they would consider it suicide to try.

The SOG told me we were still pounding through the storm at 11 knots. The wind was driving us east, and there would be thousands of square miles of ocean to hide. As the storm raged around me, I gripped the wheel, letting the rain wash over my face.

8

The gale abated after three hours. Like a miracle, the cover of clouds, filled with lightning and screaming winds, vanished, leaving the stars to watch over. The wind shifted after the front passed. Now, a northerly breeze that my anemometer measured at 18 knots left me on a beam reach.

Once the helm stopped fighting me, I set the autopilot and moved to fully raise the main and jib. Carina's hull picked up a few knots with the added sail area.

Allie was curled up in the v-berth, hiding from the storm. I knew she wasn't asleep, but I didn't want to bother her yet.

My arms hooked under the man still hanging by his right foot on the companionway steps. With some effort, I hoisted him into the cockpit. The second man lay sprawled on the floor of the cabin. A pool of blood had run starboard and congealed over the last few hours.

The hatches remained closed during the storm, and the cabin was hot and sticky. The smell of the blood reminded me of an old chicken slaughtering plant. Once I moved the second man into the cockpit, I climbed back down and opened all the hatches.

"Is the storm over?" Allie asked from my berth.

"Yeah, I think we have smooth sailing for a bit."

"What about those men?"

I wasn't sure whether she meant the two dead men or the ones left on the island.

"I'll have it cleaned up in a bit," I told her, referring to the corpses.

"No, the others."

"I don't think they can follow us. The storm covered us as we escaped. There are too many directions we might have taken, and that will leave a lot of water they would need to cover to search for us."

She nodded. "Where are we?"

That was an answer I hadn't deciphered yet. "I don't know yet."

Allie remained silent.

"Rest," I told her. "The cabin should cool down now. I'll figure out where we can go from here."

I turned to climb up to the cockpit when she asked, "Do you really think they were after me?"

"If not, it's a big coincidence."

She sobbed in the dark. "Those men. Captain Rojas, Ortiz, Manuel. Did they kill them all?"

"I don't know, Allie."

"It's all my fault," she whimpered.

"Rest," I repeated. Nothing I said would assuage her guilt. Allie needed to dwell on it for a bit before she found the strength to accept it. Of course, it wasn't her doing. Unless there were secrets she wasn't sharing. My gut didn't think so, though.

On deck, I dropped both men off Carina's stern once I'd searched them. Between the two men, I came up with 87,000 pesos. I wasn't sure of the exact conversion rate, but it was over $4,000 if my math was close. They both carried Ruger 9 mm handguns, two knives, and their Mexican passports.

Their names were Vidal Vallejo and Toli Montez. I didn't care much what their names were. In fact, it was a safe bet these were phony passports with aliases. The only thing I'd remember would be their faces. Those were imprinted like a picture in a file stuck in a drawer somewhere in my mind. Actually, that's not accurate. It was more like a slide show with random images. I'd see them again, some night when melancholy struck and sleep didn't.

That's not regret, though.

Regret is one of those emotions that can easily confuse a person. It implies I think my actions could have found a better outcome. Just because that was true, didn't mean my choice was wrong either. Sometimes, one has to react to the information available.

Regret is often mistaken for grief, which was the confusion Allie was under. She deemed the deaths of Rojas and his men as her fault, that if she'd not been on the island, they would be spared. It's true. Had we gone on to Belize or made landfall in Honduras, the cartel wouldn't have shown up.

But regret, in my humble opinion, requires a level of foreknowledge. I certainly had no idea that Allie might be a target. Which meant, with the information at my disposal, my actions were the best course to take.

The two men that now floated in the wake of *Carina* weren't things I could avoid. Between us, they were the only ones with foreknowledge. Their regret, if they had a second to feel it, might be their underestimation of the target.

I'd see their faces again, but those images won't evoke remorse. Just sadness; grief that a small chunk of my soul followed them when I dumped their corpses into the sea.

Once I came out of my thoughts, I removed a bucket from the aft locker. A 10-foot line is attached to the handle, and I tossed the bucket off the stern. With the rope, I reeled the bucket back aboard. While I installed a pump to bring water from the sea directly into the cockpit, this method was a quick way to grab just a small amount of water without having to wait for the pump to prime.

With the pail of salt water, I climbed below deck and cleaned up the blood on the cabin's sole. Once the sticky mess thinned, I rinsed it off, letting the water flow into the bilge to be pumped out later.

I tossed the bucket again and dragged it back to rinse any blood in the cockpit out the scuppers that drain out the stern.

Finally, I dropped onto the cockpit seat and took a breath. I checked my watch. It was almost dawn.

My attention turned to the chart plotter. We were only 230 miles off Jamaica. At our present speed, we would arrive in 12 hours.

It was a gamble. From the Swan Islands, there were only a few places to make landfall quickly. Jamaica was one. If the Soria men got any information from the Hondurans, they might find out my ultimate destination was Belize. Of course, anywhere on the coast of Central America was fair game, too.

But Jamaica offered tourism. A perfect place to blend in with thousands of cruise ship visitors. More importantly, an international airport where Allie can find her way back to Toronto safely. Assuming Toronto was a safe place.

It bothered me. The phone call to her company. A company whose CEO and owner died only days ago in an accident, and then Banyan Freight's jet crashes with, what I would guess, is the heir to the empire.

There were several valid reasons the cartel might attack the Hondurans. I wasn't aware of how or what influence the Sorias or anyone had on the drug trade through Honduras. Something that had nothing to do with Allie could have brought the attack on.

But it's all coincidental. I hate coincidences. Sure, they occur, but they aren't reliable. There's never an explanation.

No, everything comes back to Allie. Or, at least, Banyan Freight.

The type of business a cartel might have with a freight corporation was obvious. Transportation, smuggling, or storage.

My eyes glanced at the cabin. Questions lingered in my mind. Why try to kill the CEO and his daughter? Did some partnership deal collapse, and this was just a clean-up job? How much did Allie know?

That might be the difference between feeling regret and grief over the deaths of Captain Rojas and his men. If she was hiding her involvement with the cartel, the dead men on the island would actually be her fault. Which begged a question: How far would I go to help her?

The answer to that wasn't forthcoming, yet.

I double-checked our heading. Since I got only a couple hours of sleep on the beach, I rested for a few minutes. With the radar activated, it would alert me if anything came within five miles of us. That reassurance allowed me to let my eyes close.

When I woke up, the sun had already risen, and the eastern horizon burned with yellow, reflecting off the water ahead. It was enough of a nap to energize me, but not so much energy that I couldn't justify some coffee.

Allie was asleep now, still curled in the v-berth. I lit the burner on the alcohol stove and started the kettle. There were still some oranges I picked up in the Caymans, and I needed to finish them. Most countries frown on bringing fresh fruit from other islands for fear of contaminating their crops with some unknown pest from another part of the world. More than once, I've dumped fresh fruit and sometimes meat before I'm allowed entry into a port. Best to finish it all before I get there.

As I peeled my orange, I turned to face aft, tired of squinting into the sun. There was nothing on the horizon, meaning I had plenty of time to enjoy my orange and watch the trail left behind *Carina*. When the first dorsal fin surfaced in the wake, I straightened up. Two more followed suit, and within seconds, three dolphins were jumping and splashing less than 10 yards off the stern.

The creatures played for several minutes before darting off below the surface. It was almost seven, and in most parts of this time zone, people were scurrying off to work in cubicles or construction sites. The only sights they get is the woman in the next lane, drinking coffee and applying lipstick at 45 miles an hour.

Dolphins are a regular reminder of why I choose to be out here.

The kettle whistled, and I climbed below to finish making the coffee. With a French press filled with coffee grounds and hot water, I returned to my seat. The horizon was still clear.

We should arrive in Jamaica in the late afternoon. Today would be one of those days filled with nothing but blue. Those were my favorite. So, I poured my coffee and looked for more dolphins.

The morning passed with no more visits from playful porpoises, but a few flying fish made an appearance off the port. Allie stirred around noon. The emotional drain must have been exhausting. I was glad she slept so long. The two of us needed to talk, and if my worst suspicions were true, it would become uncomfortable on this tiny boat.

"What time is it?" she asked when she opened the doors.

"Close to lunchtime."

"I'm so sorry," she mumbled. "You didn't have to be up here alone."

"There are a couple of oranges down there, but I think the coffee is cold. You are welcome to start some more," I told her, ignoring her comment.

"I'll just have some water," she told me.

She climbed up on deck with a water bottle and an orange.

"Allie," I began, "we need to talk."

She stared at me. Her eyes were hard to read. Did she know what I was going to say?

"I've been thinking," I continued. "What business does the cartel have with Banyan Freight?"

Allie's head shook. "None. Nothing that I know."

"How involved are you in the business?"

She leaned back, but as she did, she situated herself so that her focus was on me, not the endless waves of blue behind me. "Not much. Dad ran it. I'm the youngest. Sara was the Vice-President. She had the Princeton degree in business. Dad figured she would be his successor."

"Why not you?" I asked.

"Sara is nine years older than me. By the time I gradu-ated high school, she already had her M.B.A. and worked in the office."

Allie had never told me her age. I guessed she was in her mid-20s, meaning, if she went to college, she should have been out by now.

"What do you do then?"

She shrugged. "I'm the black sheep. The day-to-day stuff bores me. I started working there when I graduated, but my job was mostly PR crap. I did nothing but travel to our different offices. It was a made-up job to let his little girl travel and feel justified."

"You keep saying 'was,'" I commented.

"After my sister's accident, I tried to take a more active role."

"Allie, I'm sorry, but what exactly happened to your sister?"

She inhaled a deep breath. "No one's sure. She was found on a trail in the Algonquin Park, outside of Toron-to. It looked like she fell and hit her head."

"Was she hiking?" I asked.

"She did jog there a lot." There was something about her tone that was hinting at doubt.

"But?" I questioned, hoping to pull more out of it.

"Sara jogged three days a week. In high school, she tore her ACL. Even with surgery, it would start to ache if she over-exerted it. So, she only jogged three days, trying to leave a recovery day in between. But the day before her accident, she and I went jogging."

"It was out of character to go two days in a row?" I asked.

Her body language showed a lack of commitment as her head swayed. She replied, "The thing is sometimes she did jog back-to-back. If her schedule got interrupted by the weather or work."

She paused.

"Or if her sister wanted to jog with her?" I suggested.

Allie's head nodded. "It was my idea to jog the day we went."

"And you think somehow it affected her accident?"

She shrugged.

Math might not be my strong suit, but Sara's fall would make three tragic accidents to befall Banyan Freight.

My eyes locked with hers. "Let's talk about the cartel."

"What about them?"

With a heavy sigh, I asked, "Do you have any involvement with them?"

Her face paled. "No!" she emphasized.

"Within a year, the entire family behind Banyan Freight has experienced tragic accidents that resulted in your father's death, your sister's condition, and two near-death experiences for you. I don't like the sound of that."

"What do you mean?" she asked incredulously.

"There is a consistent behavior among drug cartels. People that cross them become expendable, and expendable people don't live too long in that world."

Her brow furrowed. "You think we crossed the Soria Cartel, and now, they are gunning for us?"

I didn't answer. Her sister's accident was ten months ago. The next two incidents are less than a week apart. The only man I knew in a drug cartel wouldn't wait ten months to finish his business, especially if he knew right where to find his targets. Yet, the cartel was definitely on the island.

"It's important," I began, "if you knew of any business your father had with the Soria family, you tell me about it. We need an idea of what to expect."

"There's nothing. At least, nothing I know that connects to drugs."

"But?" I asked again, hoping for the same result as earlier.

"My father wasn't planning to go back to the Panama office for another month. He changed his plans at the last minute. He said it was something with the shipyard union down there."

"That could be something else."

"Not drugs, though," she insisted. "I know he wouldn't do that."

Her idealization of her father wasn't new. Most people have no idea the lines their loved ones crossed. A freight company made an ideal smuggling venue. Especially a company as big as Banyan. Those containerships carried hundreds of shipping containers each. With hundreds of ships on the ocean at any one time, the potential to smuggle contraband was enormous. There was no way any customs office could logistically search every container. Bribes could prevent the rest.

Her expression was honest unless she was a pathological criminal. If that ended up being the case, I might need to reexamine my instincts.

"Why would the cartel want the leadership of Banyan Freight killed?" I asked. "Could they have threatened your father? 'Do our business or else.'"

"He never said."

A father never would. Why scare your daughter if you can handle it yourself?

I watched her face. Every muscle was taut with determination. If she were lying, she was better trained than half the intelligence officers I'd encountered.

Leaning back, I took her at her word. Which only left the same questions unanswered.

9

"The problem is her passport is at the bottom of the ocean," I tried to explain to the Jamaican immigration officer on the dock. "We have to get her to the embassy to get another."

The rotund black man wore a crisp white tunic which appeared to me to be wool. I couldn't fathom how he wasn't sweating when my hair was already dripping after ten minutes out of the ocean breeze.

"Sir, I cannot let Ms. Tremblay into the country without the proper identification," he repeated.

I wasn't trying to argue with the man. His point was valid. Legally, Allie had no way to prove who she was. Had we been able to reach out through the proper channels, the situation could be easily rectified. Allie pointed that fact out twice since we got in line.

After the second time, I reminded her when she called her office the last time the armed men swarmed us. She relented, and now we were hoping there was a loophole we could slide through. The easiest thing would have been to send Allie ashore somewhere else. Then I'd enter through legal means. However, since *Beth* was still sitting on a sandy beach on Swan Island and Allie would rather go to a Jamaican prison than swim in the ocean, the only option was to tie up to the cruiser dock in Montego Bay.

"I understand that, sir. What can we do to facilitate her entrance? We can't access the embassy without entering the country, and there is no way to get a copy of her passport without the embassy."

"Wait here," the official ordered.

Allie shifted on her feet nervously. Since our current predicament left us between a rock and a hard place, we concocted a story that didn't mention the plane crash or trip to the Swan Islands yet. Both tales might generate a frenzy, leaving us in the middle of a "Breaking News" report on CNN. Instead, I explained to the immigration officer how Allie dropped her purse off the boat while we were underway. The only thing I could do to back it up was offer her up as the klutz that only these things happen to.

The Jamaican immigration officer returned with an older man. From the cut of his uniform, this was a superior official.

"Ms. Tremblay?" the older man inquired.

"Yes," Allie responded.

"If you'll come with me," he ordered.

Allie gave me a quizzical look. I just nodded, saying, "I'll wait here."

"No, sir," the man corrected. "You may proceed through. Wait on the other side of the entry point."

"Yes, sir," I acknowledged as he led Allie away.

It didn't seem likely that they'd arrest her. These kinds of things must happen all the time. The first officer regarded my passport.

"Did you have anything to declare?" he asked.

"No, sir," I responded. "What are they going to do with her?"

"She will be fine, sir. They will call the Canadian embassy to verify her identification and arrange for a replacement passport."

After thanking the officer, I walked through the doors of the large portico where the immigration lines wound around the stanchions toward the booth. Once I was back outside, the breeze from the ocean cooled my skin.

While I waited, I leaned against a breadfruit tree. Two young boys no older than eight ran up to me, carrying a bag of mangoes and oranges. Neither of them wore a shirt or shoes, just dirty corduroy pants cut off above the knee.

The cotton threads that once were white were brown from the dust.

"Fruit Mister! Fruit!" they exclaimed.

The mangoes appeared overripe, but the oranges were still fresh.

"How much?" I asked.

"Fi' dollas for da bag!" one blurted out.

"Five?" I questioned. "Those mangoes are all mushy. Let's call it three."

"Four?" the other countered, holding up four grubby fingers.

"Four seems fair," I agreed. Most of the tourist areas like Montego Bay happily accept American dollars. They cater to the cruise ship clientele. No point making the ugly Americans wait in line to exchange their green bills for the brightly colored currency of the island. The Americans don't have an excuse not to buy if there's no need to use local money.

The boys grinned as they nodded. Before I got off *Carina*, I stashed four stacks of ones in my front pocket. Each stack was only $20 worth of ones, but it made it easy to pull just one-dollar bills out without flashing all my cash. I stored the bigger bills in my wallet.

I peeled the four dollars off one stack and handed it to the boy with the fruit. He greedily snatched it and passed the bag to me. The entire collection of fruit probably cost the kids less than a buck, if they didn't just collect them directly from the trees or, judging by the mangoes, the ground.

"Can you answer a question?" I asked the boy as he stuffed the four bills down the front of his pants.

"Yeah, Mister."

"Which way is the Toby Inn?"

He cocked his head and stared at me. My fingers peeled another dollar off the stack and stuck it forward. Like a coiled snake snapping at its prey, his hand shot up and took the bill.

"Mister, you gotta take a taxi. It's too far to walk."

"But where is it?" I asked, feigning to take my dollar back.

"Dat way!" he exclaimed as he jerked the bill down to his waist.

"Thank you." I already knew where I was going.

The boys giggled and ran off. I watched them run with bare feet across the rocky yard as if it was sand. As they scampered away, I tested the mangoes. They oozed ripe juice through the thick skin when I gave them a squeeze. After deciding they weren't worth keeping, I tossed them into the bushes where the birds could feast.

The orange, on the other hand, was firm, and after peeling it, I found the fruit tasted deliciously fresh. I guessed the boys plundered a local tree. My back slid down the trunk of the tree until I was resting on the dirt. The juice from the orange ran down my fingers as I pulled the sections apart to eat each one.

After an hour, I removed the skin of another. Just as delicious. By the time I finished that one, I spotted Allie wandering out the exit alone. She was looking around as three women swarmed her, hocking dresses and hand-woven fans and sandals. Allie waved them off, and I rose to my feet to rescue her.

"Excuse me," I announced as I bowled through the women. "We aren't interested right now."

"Where you stay?" a woman holding a dress made in China and designed to look as if it was authentic Caribbean attire. We'd end up seeing several vendors with the same or similar style. "You buy from me later. I here all day."

"'Member me! 'Member me!" another shouted.

"Later," I boomed in a baritone.

The women scattered, but not without a few more last-ditch pitches. "Promise me," the dress lady called. "You buy from me later."

I waved her off as I put my hand on the small of Allie's back, guiding her to the street.

"That's a lot," she muttered.

"Welcome to Jamaica," I told her. "Want an orange?"

"Where'd you get these?" she asked, pulling the last one from the bag.

"A couple of used car salesmen hit me up."

"Where are we going?" she asked.

"There's a decent hotel at the end of the main strip."

She glanced around the street as we found the taxi queue.

"Ever been to Jamaica?" I asked.

"Yeah, I've only gone to some resorts in Negril and Ocho Rios."

A smile crossed my face. "This might be a fresh experience for you. We are staying on the down low."

Her right eyebrow lifted. I almost made a snarky comment about her being a princess, but I caught it before it passed my lips. It wouldn't have been fair. So far, other than the fear of water, which I could forgive, she had gone along with the ride without a single complaint. Even the fear of water hadn't held her back.

The first taxi was a gray Peugeot coupe. The word "taxi" was hand-painted on both front doors. A middle-aged man leaned against the fender talking with agitated animation to the driver of the second car in line. From a distance, it appeared as if the two were about to exchange fists, but laughter erupted. They cajoled each other as we approached.

The driver of the Peugeot straightened when he saw two tourists seeking transportation. "You need a ride?" he bellowed in his thick Jamaican accent.

"Yes, please," I responded. The other drivers waiting perked up.

"My name is Solomon," he greeted as he opened the door for Allie. "Where are ya going?"

"Downtown," I offered vaguely. No point announcing to everyone in earshot where we were staying.

Before he could open the rear passenger door, I scooted around the trunk and climbed into the front passenger's seat. It wasn't necessarily an alpha male thing, I told myself. More OpSec. Operational Security. It's second nature to me, thanks to the United States Marine Corps. Particularly one sergeant at Parris Island that pounded it into my brain.

Solomon was, like most Jamaicans I've met, friendly, chatty, and a fireball of energy. The country is poor, and its people know that the only money to be made is off the "rich" tourists that visit. Somewhere in time, the lesson taught them was to strike fast, deal hard, and never accept "no" as an answer.

"Would you like a tour?" Solomon offered before his door slammed shut. "Dere's Rose Hall, de market, mehbe de beach?"

"Just take us down to Gloucester," I told him, resting my elbow on the open window.

"Yessir." He fired off the response. "Where'ya from?"

Allie and I had already discussed our answers. So it rolled off her tongue as she responded, "Chicago."

"Da Cubs!" he exclaimed.

She smiled, less enthusiastically than most Chicagoans might do at the mention of the Cubs.

"She's more a Sox fan," I told him.

Solomon grinned. His smile was wide and white. "Da Sox ain't got nutting on da Cubs."

I made a face of surrender and replied, "You're preaching to the choir."

He chuckled. "So where can I take ya lovely folks. Da Rose Hall is very pretty. Lots of flowers."

"Just drop us at the Toby Inn."

"Ahhh, da Toby. Yessir."

The little gray Peugeot lurched forward as Solomon slapped the stick into first gear. A sign warned that "sleeping police" were ahead.

"What does that mean?" Allie asked.

The cab bounded over a tall speed bump, and I was sure Solomon was attempting to catch some air between the tires and the ground.

He howled with laughter. "Dat is de sleeping police!"

I exhaled with mirth and stole a glance at Allie in the back seat. Her body was twisted to glimpse the speed bump we just crossed.

"Why do they call them sleeping police?" she asked Solomon as she turned back.

"Cause dey sleepin' on da job," he explained.

Solomon's foot pressed down on the gas as he shifted into fourth gear. He turned back to smile at Allie as he weaved around four different cars, occasionally honking for no apparent reason, followed by a friendly wave. If there wasn't a friendly gesture, Solomon would shout out his window. "Gid outta da way, mon!"

The ride to the hotel only lasted five minutes, partly because Solomon didn't slow for traffic. He just drove around it. Stop signs were only suggestions, and at one light, he made a "Harumph!" as he sped through the red light without looking either way.

I half expected him to skid to a stop in front of the inn. Instead, he slid into a tight spot on the curb with one fluid motion.

"Thank you, Solomon," I told him as I paid his fare with an American 20-dollar bill.

"Got no change, Mister Cubbie."

"Don't need none, Solomon," I informed him as I shut the door.

"Mister Cubbie," he shouted back.

My head stuck inside the open passenger window.

"You need a ride anywheres, call dis number," he handed me a handwritten business card. I could decipher the name Solomon, but only because I knew what his name was. The numbers were clear enough.

"Thank you, Solomon."

"Irie," he whistled as the car launched out of the parking spot.

I could hear the cabbie shouting out, "Need a ride!" as he whipped down Gloucester Avenue.

"That was quite a ride," Allie commented.

With a smile, I remarked, "I told you this was going to be a fresh experience for you."

10

"We could have gone to the Ritz," Allie pointed out as I opened the door to the bungalow style room.

The Toby Inn was a modest motel that didn't offer all-inclusive anything. There was a pool in the courtyard and most of the rooms opened onto the space. The tiled roof and stucco siding were reminiscent of most tropical buildings.

"I'm just saying," she continued. "I have an account there."

I stepped inside the room, heading directly for the air conditioner hanging on the wall.

"You have an account?" I questioned as I clicked the cool button. The box whirred for five seconds before cold air blasted out.

"Banyan Freight," she answered matter-of-factly.

"What happens when the Ritz reaches out to Banyan Freight about their guest."

Her right eyebrow lifted. I'd noted that facial tic happened when something tested her boundaries. "Fine," she muttered. "This isn't bad."

"All we have to do is wait for your passport without getting into any trouble. After that, you can fly home to Toronto and figure out what the hell is happening with your company."

She was still wearing a pair of shorts and a tank top that was left on my boat by another woman. However, she'd been in the same outfit since the plane crash.

"I desperately want a shower and some clean clothes," she announced as she flopped back on the bed. The springs in the mattress, worn from years of use, bounced her more than she expected. A giggle slipped out, and I couldn't resist smiling.

"Tell you what," I suggested. "I can see if I can find you something to wear right now while you take a shower."

"Oh, Chase, that would be great."

"Don't expect too much. The hotel had a gift shop, so I'm sure there's a t-shirt with something tacky and vulgar on it."

She pulled the tank top up over her head as she sprang to her feet. "Make sure it's good and tasteless," she told me.

As I watched her walk topless to the bathroom, I offered, "Maybe something sheer and see-through."

Her head popped out of the bathroom door. She shook her hair free, running her fingers through the knotted mess. "Good, I can't wait to hit the town like that."

"Keep the door locked," I warned her. "I have a key."

"Yes, sir," she retorted as I walked into the courtyard.

About a month ago, I was in Jamaica before heading to the Cayman Islands. I spent most of the time anchored near Ocho Rios, enjoying the beaches filled with scores of single women on girls' trips. It sounds lecherous, which it isn't. The most I did was share a few pitchers of daiquiris with a group of former Wisconsin State sorority girls celebrating a 20-something reunion. I couldn't remember the name of the sorority, but I enjoyed their company, not to mention their karaoke skills.

Before that, it was nearly 20 years ago when I visited the country. The people were like most island people. They portrayed a happy face. Got to look good for the pictures. I wondered how many people had photographs of the two fruit salesmen placarded up on their social media page. The caption won't even have their names.

When I stop in places like this, it makes me sad. The image we portrayed must surely appall them. Like invaders, we trample through their homeland with no regard for them. To us, the women selling cheap made-in-China dresses, designed to appear handmade by locals, are novelties; things to snap pictures of. These are really hard-working people desperate to buy food in a place where the visitors dictate the prices. Ugly Americans, indeed.

I'm probably just as guilty. Our culture bred the nonchalance of excess into all of America. We want something, we get something, because we deserve something. It's bullshit, and I'm ashamed of myself for it.

My attention snapped forward as the door to the front office opened. A statuesque figure stepped through the opening as I neared. The woman in front of me wore a red strap that must have been a bikini, but she wore that string well. In fact, in square inches, I think her cat eye sunglasses resting on the bridge of her nose covered more skin.

I couldn't place her age, but immediately I recognized the European gait. She looked to be in her 40s, but the back of her hand was the only place that showed her years. If she wasn't all natural, then whatever doctor did her work was a genius. The only unnatural thing about her was the dye job in her hair. The color was actually perfect, but it was too precise. Of course, nine out of ten guys passing her right now wouldn't even know she had hair.

I need to come back here. Sorority karaoke was fun, but...the thought trailed off as I stepped into the front office.

The gift shop was being generous when it called itself that. The six shelves in a closet held cheap trinkets emblazoned with "Montego Bay," "Irie, Mon," or "Jamaica Me Crazy." Two hanger rods held an assortment of cheesy shirts. I picked out the classiest of the bunch. It was screen printed with a caricature of Bob Marley. The joint sticking out of his mouth wasn't the focal point, so it made it the nicest. The only shorts they offered were pink with "Irie" printed on the butt. Much like the gift shop itself, calling them shorts was an overstatement. I've seen women's underwear that covered more.

The woman at the front desk totaled up the purchase. Since I paid with American currency for the room, I already knew she had no problem with it. She watched me closely as she counted the money.

"Also, we are expecting a package tomorrow," I told her. "It will come from the Canadian Embassy in Kingston."

"Yes, sir."

"Do you have a map of the area?"

She handed me a receipt and pointed at a table behind me. Maps printed in color on legal-sized paper of the area called Hip Strip, were stacked on the table. I folded two and carried them with me.

As I crossed the courtyard, the European woman, who had found a chaise lounge next to the pool, shifted her eyes over her sunglasses. She offered me a half-smile of greeting. I gave her my $10-gosh-ain't-you-pretty smile. She pushed the glasses up on the bridge of her nose as she turned her head up to the sun.

The Toby Inn still used actual keys to open the rooms. The single key jangled from the red plastic tab as I pulled it from my shorts. I unlocked the door to hear the shower running. Allie's new clothes landed on the bed closest to the bathroom.

I flopped onto the other bed, crossing my feet as my head sank into the pillow. The room was clean, but needed some updating. The walls were almost a florescent mustard, if that was even possible. It was the color only used in the tropics. Although, even in the islands, this shade seemed out of place.

The ceiling was yellowed from years of allowing guests to smoke in the rooms. The sign on the door now forbade it, but no one had painted over the white ceiling. Unless decades of smoke bled through the whitewash.

The wall let out a groaning belch as the shower stopped. A minute passed before the door opened a crack.

"Chase, you back?" Allie asked.

"Want me to hand you some clothes?" I offered.

Without answering me, she stepped out with a white towel cinched just over her nipples. Her hair was damp, but she'd managed to rake her fingers through it to allow it to fall, somewhat untangled, over her shoulders.

"These look lovely," she remarked as she studied my selection.

"I warned you."

She released the towel, letting it fall free in one hand. Despite the urge not to do so, I diverted my attention. However, it was not before I caught a glimpse.

"I hope you have something as formal for dinner tonight."

"Dang," I quipped. "My wife-beater collection is still on the boat."

"They better be adequately stained," she retorted.

"They come in two colors: white with grease stains and white with ketchup stains."

As she pulled the shorts over her legs, she joked, "Don't turn me on like that."

"Ta-da!" she announced, spinning clockwise to show off her outfit.

"You look *irie*," I told her.

"Is that the correct usage?" she asked.

I shrugged.

She slipped into the pair of flip-flops left on *Carina* by the former owner of the tank top Allie wore earlier. "What's the plan?" she asked.

"I guess we can see the town," I suggested. "I told the front desk to expect something from the embassy. I imagine it's going to arrive tomorrow at the earliest."

"Can we find something else I can wear?" she requested.

"Come on," I told her, waving the map I picked up in the office. "I have a map."

From the inn, we walked east along Gloucester Avenue. The rest of the drivers on the road operated their vehicles with the same devil-may-care attitude that Solomon had. Horns beeped from every direction as drivers warned everyone they were changing lanes. From what I saw, the rules of the road were simple: I'm going there, get out of my way.

We crossed the street with more care than I'd ever considered necessary. It was everything my kindergarten teacher warned. Pedestrians didn't have the right-of-way. If anything, the cars thought they were orange cones to weave through.

"That's insane," Allie acknowledged after we ran across the four lanes during a three second gap of traffic.

"Pineapple!" an old woman howled from beneath the shade of a palm tree. The lady was in her 90s. Her figure was thin and frail, but hooked on the frail elbow of her left arm, she toted a basket with at least ten pineapples.

"Pineapple!" she called again through a toothless grin. "Wanna pineapple?"

"How much?" I asked.

"Ett dollas," she responded. "American dollas."

I handed her eight dollars. The old woman selected a large one from the top of her basket. From a cloth sack strung over her shoulder, she pulled two plastic bags and a large paring knife. We watched as she wrapped the bag over each hand. Once the plastic covered her fingers, she carved into the prickly skin. The green top and skin filled one bag. When the skin was off the fruit, the only thing visible was the yellow flesh. The woman sliced the fruit into spears. When she finished, the point of the knife stabbed into the fibrous core so she could pull it from the bag. With one hand, she tied up the skin and scraps in one bag before dropping it in her basket. Her other hand folded the top of the bag of fresh-cut fruit and handed it to Allie.

"Thank you," Allie told her.

The old woman grinned her toothless smile and waddled after another group of tourists. "Pineapple!" she shouted after them.

"She never touched the pineapple," Allie noted as she looked into the container. "That's insane."

My fingers dipped into the clear bag, extracting a spear. The juice ran down my chin as I bit into it.

"Oh my gosh," Allie exclaimed as she took a bite. "That's amazing."

"Hard to get fresh pineapple in Canada, isn't it?"

She muttered something as she filled her mouth with another bite. I grabbed another before guiding her past some street vendors selling sugar cane, fruit, and some type of jerky.

We took a trail up the hill where a sign read "Straw Market" and pointed up the hill.

The straw market was a maze of tents, huts, and shacks cobbled together with whatever the shopkeepers could find. It was like a flea market of crafts and clothes. There were plenty of duplicate "Irie" shirts, lots of Bob Marley images, carvings of dolphins, rays, and birds, tropical dresses, and a plethora of marijuana themed products. Like the dress the woman tried to sell us at the docks, most of this stuff came to the island from overseas. As we wound our way through the labyrinth, shopkeepers stepped out and focused their sights on the easy target, Allie.

"You need dresses?"

"I have stuff. Come see my shop!"

"Hey missus. Lemme show you my store."

While they crowded around her, each attempting to drag a part of her to their respective stores, a few realized the vultures had picked over that wildebeest. While they must assume the women do the most shopping, I was being eyed like prey.

"*Ganja!*" one man hissed at me with a lecherous wink.

"You like belts?" a woman asked.

Another older woman gripped my hand, tugging me toward her tent. "Come wid me," she rasped.

I pulled my hand free. "Wait up," I announced, pushing away from the crowd to save Allie.

"We'll look at everything." My voice raised over the din of the vendors. "Back up!"

The crowd reacted, stepping back in unison, but remaining within shouting distance. Their squawks repeating, "Come here" and "See my shop."

"Holy shit," Allie mumbled when I pulled her against me.

"Never done the markets?" I asked.

She shook her head.

While the vendors were overbearing, the sight was surreal. It was a dog-eat-dog world. The competition for tourist dollars was fierce. In fact, I was certain at least one woman hissed a warning at her neighbor, saying, "I saw her first."

"Come on," I urged Allie into one shop.

The woman greeted us with enthusiasm. "Welcome," she announced, waving her hands over the three walls of wooden pallets holding dresses with intricate stitching of flowers and birds.

As Allie ran her fingers over the material, the shopkeeper glared at her neighbors hovering six or seven feet from the opening. It was a warning and a gloat. She had the customer.

From the direction we came, another couple wandered into the maze. The horde descended on them with their shouts.

"I like this one," Allie commented to me.

"You like," the old woman stated. "Tirdy dollas."

Allie was about to agree when I interjected. "Twenty."

The woman feigned insult. "Twinny fi'."

My head shook. "Twenty."

The shopkeeper heaved a sigh. "Okay, okay. Twinny."

Allie took the dress from her as I offered her the money. Holding it up against herself, she modeled the dress. It was a coral color with lacy fringes on the sleeves and a hyacinth embroidered on the breast. It was the perfect beach dress.

"If I could change now, I would," she told me.

"You really don't like my taste, huh?"

Without answering, she leaned over and kissed my cheek before bounding out of the shop.

"You li' hats?" the shopkeeper asked me, waving her hand over a display of straw hats.

"No, thank you," I replied as I made a graceful exit.

The throngs of vendors still circled, but with new shoppers coming into their lair, the attentions were divided. Allie carried her purchase as she peeked in the different shacks—each keeper offering the grand tour.

We exited down the back way to Gloucester again. Allie bought two more dresses, although she didn't enjoy negotiating the prices. The last shop ended up throwing in a Panama Jack knockoff fedora with her dress.

Allie rested the hat on my head. "It'll keep the sun off your face."

Considering my face was always a dark tan from the sun, it seemed a little too late. However, Allie was enjoying herself, and for the first time, I forgot what happened on the last island.

11

T he sun was setting, but from where we were sitting, we could only see the orange sky. Meat sizzled a few feet away over an open pit. Long metal skewers held chunks of chicken and pork. The pit master at the Pork Pit was dripping sweat as he rotated the meat under the thatched roof.

"It's not the most sanitary," Allie commented.

"Not that different from cooking burgers on a grill," I retorted.

"I guess," she admitted. "It smells amazing."

A skinny older man, who wore a tank top and shorts, sprinkled seasoning over a fresh skewer before placing it on the grills. White hot embers heated the air under the portico to over 120 degrees. As the man joked with another, he moved down the pit, keeping the food from overcooking.

I'd never sampled the Pork Pit, but it was a world-renowned must-stop when in Montego Bay. If the opportunity was here, I wasn't about to miss it.

Allie was less sure. While she was used to the all-inclusive lifestyle, she'd tried everything today. For most of the day, we meandered down the sidewalk, exploring the stores and shops along the way. Since I enjoy the sand and surf most days and Allie would never enjoy it, we skipped the beach. Jimmy Buffett's Margaritaville, too. Not that there's anything wrong with the colorful bar, but I like the local dives. So, we sampled fresh sugar cane and a mango, carved up by the same woman who sold us the pineapple earlier. Now, she was laden with mangoes in her basket.

We sat at a tall table in the shade. An ice cold glass bottle of Coca-Cola sat in front of each of us, sweating rings of water onto the table. The bent tops rested next to the sodas. After walking through the Jamaican heat all day, I expected these two drinks to vanish before our food showed up. I took another swallow. Next to a frosty bottle of beer, nothing beats an ice cold Coca-Cola in a glass bottle. I steer clear of sodas most of the time, and after seeing how many plastic bottles float on the surface of the ocean, I refuse to drink anything out of plastic. But an icy Coke is hard to resist.

A thin girl pushed through the door. I doubted she was even 14. She sported a Justin Bieber t-shirt and long braided hair. In each hand she carried a paper plate, piled with chicken, pork, rice, and a fried bread called festival.

The two forks she offered us were cheap plastic ones that stood no chance against the chunks of meat.

"I hope you don't find me uncouth," I commented as I picked up the chicken.

Allie grinned and grabbed her piece, stuffing it in her mouth.

"Oh wow," she mumbled.

We ordered two more Coca-Colas and decided the next round needed to be Red Stripes. When I reached a stopping point, there was still half a plate of food.

"We should have shared," Allie told me.

"Live and learn," I replied, still picking at my food.

"I'm glad we have a two-mile hike back to the hotel."

I took a sip of the Red Stripe and watched the people file past the restaurant. The influx of cruise ship passengers hit about nine in the morning, but by now they were all safely aboard their giant boats. The locals began filling in the gaps left by the cruisers. Now Montego Bay would come to life a little more. There were still plenty of visitors to plunder, but the ripe ones disappeared until nine tomorrow morning.

"I've been thinking," Allie commented as her fork stirred the rice. "Could my brother-in-law be behind this?"

My mouth was full, and I swallowed as I watched her face. Her brow wrinkled as she waited for an answer.

"I'm not sure," I acknowledged. "If something happens to you, then does he get control of the company?"

"Technically, yes," she explained. "Sara was Dad's right hand, but since her accident, Steven has stepped up while I was getting my feet wet."

She continued, "I don't know for sure what Dad had in his will. I'd guess the control of the company would go to Sara and me, but with Sara's condition, I don't know."

"Would Steven inherit from Sara if something happened to her?" I asked.

Allie shrugged. "I think if Sara had died before Dad, there would be less to inherit. It would still be a lot, though."

My fingers pulled a chunk of chicken off the thigh. "At this point," I started, "if you died, who gets your share of the company?"

"My will gives everything to Sara," she told me.

I nodded. "What happens if Sara dies before you?"

"I'd guess her share goes to Steven."

"No," I corrected. "If Sara dies, then you die?"

"Oh," she muttered, letting the emptiness of the question consume her for a second. Finally, she answered, "I think the shares would likely go back to the company. I'm not sure. That wasn't something we considered when I was preparing my will."

"Your death now seems to benefit Steven," I pointed out. "That doesn't mean he's guilty, though. I don't know him."

She shook her head. "I can't imagine. He's family."

I didn't want to point out that family means different things to people. On the other hand, my family shouldn't be used to judge others.

"Listen, Allie, it could be something else too. Someone else. Who was it you talked to the other day?"

"Bryan. Bryan White," she responded.

"What's his job?"

"He's Steven's assistant."

"Ah," I commented.

It didn't matter what I thought at this point. Allie found the string that she was going to tug. She knew the dynamics of her family and business far better than I would. If she came to suspect her brother-in-law, it was likely a solid suspicion.

"I think I need something stronger than Red Stripe," Allie pointed out as she swallowed the last bit of beer from her bottle.

"We passed a place on the way down here that offered a bigger variety."

"Come on," she urged me as she gathered up our plates to toss them in a metal garbage can.

We walked west on Gloucester. The streets were lined with a heavy mix of locals and visitors, most dressed for nightlife. Steel drums echoed off the wall, and various reggae sounds emanated from bars and clubs.

The post-cruise evening reminded me of a scene from a movie where the parents leave and the teenagers immediately pull out the party. Makeshift DJ stands were dragged onto the sidewalk to blare music to those in the vicinity. Since we were some of the few non-cruisers that stayed on the island, we were lucky to see the change. While there were still plenty of stereotypical grifters working through the throngs of visitors, compared to a few hours ago–it was almost nonexistent.

"How about here?" Allie pointed at a sign for The Pelican Grill. The restaurant boasted a bar with grainy pictures of daiquiris and other fruity cocktails. A blown-up picture of a slice of key lime pie promised it was the best on the island.

"I want some pie," Allie told me.

"How do you have room?" I questioned, feeling the jerk and festival sitting in my gut.

She smiled at me. "I always have room for pie," she promised, grabbing my hand and pulling me up the stairs to the white building.

The inside of The Pelican Grill had a simplistic design. The dining room was tiled with large white ceramic tile. Along the walls were round booths with leather seats that reminded me of a cross between a hospital cafeteria and a Shoney's Restaurant circa 1989. A hall led off to the right where music drifted out. It wasn't loud or obnoxious like so many bars. Nor was it so soft it felt like elevator music.

A hostess pointed us down the hall when Allie asked for the bar.

"Order me something fun but strong," Allie told me. "Fruity, but not frozen."

She left me to find the women's restroom, and I idled up to the bar. A Jamaican woman in her 20s was slinging drinks. The barstools were half-filled, and I found two near the end. In an attempt to differentiate the bar from the restaurant, The Pelican Grill followed the rule long established in the 50s and 60s, dim the lights in the bar while the dining room glowed like center stage at Madison Square Garden.

"Marine, eh?" A gruff voice erupted from my left.

My eyes adjusted to the lighting, and I found the source. A broad man in his 60s. He wore leathered skin as if he'd spent a lifetime in the sun. His right arm showed the faded ink. I could still read the "Fi."

"Used to be," I acknowledged.

"No one used to be a Marine," he growled. "'Nam. '69."

My hand shot out to grip his. His palm was as rough as his skin appeared, and he smelled like he had been sweating whiskey for days.

"Lewis Jagger," he sputtered.

"Chase Gordon."

"What'd ya do, Gordon?"

"Recon," I informed him.

"A badass, eh?"

"Aren't all Marines?" I quipped.

"Oorah," he announced, lifting a shot glass of whiskey to me before tossing it back.

"Milly," he called to the bartender. "Bring me and my buddy a shot."

The 20-year-old bartender poured two shots of well whiskey and set them in front of us.

Jagger lifted his glass, reciting, "Here's to cheating, stealing, fighting, and drinking. If you cheat, may you cheat death. If you steal, may you steal a woman's heart. If you fight, may you fight for a brother. If you drink, may you drink with me."

His shot glass clinked against mine before we turned them both up and slammed them down on the bar.

"Are you already finding trouble?" Allie asked as she slipped onto the stool beside me.

"Ahhh," Jagger grinned lecherously. "You have your own maiden."

"Don't we all," I commented.

His eyes glassed over a bit as he responded, "Yeah."

"Lewis Jagger, this is Allie Tremblay."

The old Marine dipped his head respectfully. "Please pardon an old drunk, sweetheart. My manners have long since eroded."

Allie smiled. "Nothing to pardon. You just have a head start."

Jagger bellowed in laughter. "You are my kinda woman. What are ya drinking?"

"What's a good Jamaican drink?" she asked.

"Milly!" Jagger shouted across the bar.

The bartender strolled over, ignoring the obnoxious nature. She was a professional, and it was obvious that Jagger was a regular. Not just a tourist here for a few days, who found his temporary bar. He was entrenched here.

"The lady wants a good Jamaican drink," he told her.

She turned to Allie, asking in a melodious accent, "Something fruity?"

Allie nodded, as Milly began mixing what looked like a Rum Runner.

"Do you live here, Lewis?" Allie asked.

"Since '87," he responded. "I have a house over in St. James."

"Are there a lot of Americans living here?" she asked.

"Oh, we have a few. Most are fresh money. Not a lot of grunts like me."

"Grunts?" she asked.

"Marines," I explained to her.

"What made you come here?" she asked.

"Eh, life's a lot simpler here. Lot of us needed something less hectic."

"You mean Marines?" she asked.

"Rejects, outcasts. Those of us that don't fit."

Allie stole a glance at me. She was wondering how different I was from Jagger. I lived on the outskirts too.

"What do you do down here?"

"I fish. Mostly. Occasionally I'll make a run to the mainland."

"What do you do that for?" she asked naively.

"Are you guys narcs?"

Allie's eyes widened. "Uh?" she stammered.

I chuckled. "No, not at all."

Jagger changed subjects slightly. "Lot of money being made down here like that. Especially us lost souls. There's a Marine up in the jungle. Flew in the Gulf War. Runs drugs up to the States. Name's Viener. Way he talks, he's a hellacious pilot. He comes down every few months with wads of greenbacks. Makes me wish I could fly."

"In the jungle?" Allie asked. "In Jamaica?"

"Sure thing, sweetheart. You think Jamaica's all beaches and bars?"

She shook her head demurely, and Jagger let out a chuckle. "You should visit him. The folks in the interior are different from the ones living in the tourist towns. Get a car and drive up to Johns Hall. You'll find a different world up there."

Milly approached the old Marine. "Lewie," she called him lovingly, "it's time to close out."

Jagger nodded begrudgingly. "Thanks, Milly." He pulled a wad of Jamaican bills from his pocket and counted off several.

"Tell Kim, 'goodnight,'" Milly told the man as he turned.

"G'night, folks," Jagger told us as he shuffled out of the bar.

Once he left, Milly told us, "Lewis is a nice man, but his girl likes to make sure he's home by nine."

"You do that?" Allie asked.

Milly responded, "He'd drink here until he can't stand if I let him. His girl, Kim, told me he can have no more than eight drinks. More than that and he gets lost. Last time, he stole a Jeep and woke up in the mountains."

"That's a good service to have," I noted.

"Lewie is just sad. I think he'd drink himself to death if he could."

"He doesn't seem sad," Allie commented.

"His wife died years ago, and he just never got over her."

"What about Kim?"

"Kim loves him, and Lewie loves her. She just isn't his wife."

"That's just sad," Allie replied.

Milly brought us a couple of fresh drinks. Allie slurped hers down and begged for another.

"Can I try the key lime pie?" she asked Milly.

As we worked our way through several rounds of Rum Runners, we talked about life. Mostly Allie's, but she'd interject a poignant question, trying to coax information out of me.

When Milly came by around two, I noticed we were the last customers hanging on. I settled up the bill and pulled a nearly limp Allie off her stool. She stumbled under the influence of rum.

Her fingers wrapped around my biceps as she steadied herself going down the steps.

"You have nice arms," she slurred as she stroked her fingers over the muscles.

"They're just arms," I told her, but she pulled close to me.

After the second time she stumbled over the sidewalk crack, I flagged down a cab. Nestled in the back seat, Allie purred as she held my arm. Her hands were cool in the humid, hot night.

The rum had done a number on me as well, just not to the same extent. Enough that I wasn't quite able to distinguish whether I was making bad decisions or not. When she kissed me, I didn't care how bad the decision was.

I'm single. She's single.

At least, I thought she was. It didn't matter. By the time the cabbie let us out in front of The Toby Inn, I knew I wanted her.

12

The knock on the door woke me up. Allie lay across my chest in the bed, her leg hooked over mine. My arm wrapped around her, and my left hand pressed against her bare back. She didn't stir, even after the third knock.

I shifted my body to move her, and in doing so, she pulled me closer.

"Where do you think you're going, mister?" she mumbled.

"Someone's knocking on the door."

"Bah," she blurted out. "They'll go away."

Before I could argue with her, I felt her lips on my chest. I lost track of the knocking as she moved against me. She straightened her back as she stared down at me with lusty eyes.

At least, now, I knew the rum wasn't the only contributing factor.

After several minutes, we rolled away from each other to catch our breath.

"Who was at the door?" she asked, panting.

My head lolled over to stare at her. "Someone wouldn't let me check."

Allie twisted around to kiss me playfully. "It was more fun to not."

"No argument there," I assured her. "Maybe your passport came."

Her mouth twisted into a half-frown.

"That's a good thing," I pointed out.

She flopped onto her back and stared at the ceiling. "I know," she admitted. "It also means I'm forced to face what's going on."

"That seems inevitable."

"Likely," she conceded. "But, why can't we just stay here in Jamaica."

"I don't have enough money to stay here forever," I explained. "Now, if we could get you over your fear of boats, there's an option."

The bed shook as she shivered at the thought of living on a boat.

"I have plenty of money," she pointed out.

"True, but until you go back you can't access it."

Her feet kicked up and down like a toddler throwing a fit. When she stopped, she looked over at me. "Would you come back with me?" she asked.

"To Toronto?"

"Yeah. Not forever, of course. Just long enough to help me find out what's going on there."

I'd never been to Toronto. The city didn't make any must-do's on my bucket list. Of course, that's only because I knew little about it.

"Sure," I agreed. "I'll need to make sure I secure *Carina* for a few weeks."

A grin spread across her mouth. "I could kiss you!" she exclaimed.

"Whoa," I interjected as she reached for me. "I need a few minutes to recover."

"Bah," she hissed, playfully pushing me away.

I swung my feet around and pulled a pair of shorts up my legs.

"Now, where are you going?" she pined.

"I'm going to check the front desk," I explained. "Back in five minutes."

"Ugh," she moaned, pulling the sheets over her head.

We had slept until almost nine. Late for me. Of course, I wasn't sure what time we finally went to sleep last night.

A young Middle-Eastern boy was behind the front desk. He looked up as I strolled into the small air-conditioned lobby.

"Did we get a package?" I asked, showing him my room key.

"Yes, sir," he acknowledged. "I tried to bring it to your room."

The boy wasn't much older than 14. Glad I didn't answer the door.

He pulled out a brown composite envelope bigger than legal size. A stamp on the front marked it "Urgent." The Canadian Embassy's address in Kingston was printed in the upper left corner.

"Thank you," I told him as I left the office.

As I crossed the courtyard, I noticed the same European woman who had been sunning herself by the pool yesterday. She was wearing more clothes than when I first saw her, but her statuesque form was unmistakable. She walked casually toward me at a slow enough gait to draw my head around. The woman's face never acknowledged me. Despite knowing that it was a ploy, my eyes followed her as she walked between the buildings toward Gloucester Avenue. She passed a dark-skinned man who barely registered in my brain. When I took a second glance, the sidewalk was empty.

Allie was in the shower when I got back to the room. Part of me wanted to join her, but like a coach once said, it's better to show up rested and ready to play.

The door latch clicked as I secured it. My fingers lifted the curtains to take a glimpse outside. The courtyard was empty. I watched for a full minute before chalking it up to my imagination.

The shower cut off, and I waited until the door opened. Allie stepped out wrapped in a towel.

"You should have joined me," she suggested.

I walked past her and pulled her close to kiss her neck. "I didn't think there was enough room."

"There's never enough room," she commented. "That's not the point."

"I think your passport arrived," I told her. My fingers caught the edge of the towel, and I whipped it off, leaving her naked in the middle of the room. "I'm stealing your towel," I quipped as I headed into the shower.

When I came out, Allie was lounging on the bed watching a soccer game.

"Can we grab some breakfast?" she asked.

"I saw a place down the street advertising an English breakfast."

Allie scrunched up her nose. "Does that include beans?"

My eyebrow lifted. "You don't have a lot of room to talk. Canadian bacon."

"Mmm, let's go," she encouraged me as I dressed.

"Grab your passport," I reminded her. "We can see about getting a flight to Canada."

She slipped the brand new document in my pocket as I locked the door.

"No pockets," she pointed out as she twirled in the new dress.

"But so cute," I amended.

"I know, right?" She bounced up and kissed my cheek.

I couldn't imagine this was the same woman I pulled from the wreckage only days ago. This one showed exuberance, and I couldn't fathom someone trying to snuff that out.

The cafe was only half a block from The Toby Inn, and they gave us a table on the raised patio overlooking Gloucester Avenue.

The coffee was local, harvested up in the mountains and roasted somewhere on the island. At least, that was the story the waitress told us. Allie ordered the full English breakfast with fried eggs and beans. When the woman offered her Canadian bacon or regular bacon, Allie sneered at me as she told her, "Canadian, please."

I opted for the American version: three eggs scrambled, three pieces of bacon, toast, and fresh fruit.

Most importantly, I ordered a pot of coffee. While we waited on our food, the two of us sat quietly sipping coffee and watching the morning pedestrian traffic. From where we were perched, I watched a big cruise ship moving into the harbor.

The city was about to be invaded.

Once our order arrived, I focused on the eggs. Every bartender has a hangover remedy, and while I wasn't suffering from one, my post-drinking habit is eggs and greasy bacon. Something about the combination clears the remnants of the night before.

Halfway through my second piece of bacon, I noticed the same man on the street that vanished at the same time the European woman did. He stood across the street, leaning against a concrete wall. His left foot lifted so the sole of his shoe was against the wall.

I had a better view of him, and it was easy to determine he was Hispanic.

Are you being paranoid, Chase?

There was no reason he couldn't be a tourist. Even a local. Surely, there was a population of Hispanics on the island. I had seen none, but that meant nothing.

The second one was back down the street toward The Toby Inn. He was under a tree. His goal was to appear nonchalant, as if he was enjoying the shade. While he appeared to be resting, possibly even napping, he lifted his head every couple of minutes, rotating between the cafe and the inn.

My eyes scanned the patio as I tried to smile at Allie. The cafe seemed clear. They were waiting for us to leave. The way the building housing the cafe had been built the structure butted against a rock wall. The only real exit was onto the street. No sneaking past them.

I sucked in a breath of air. What had we left in our room? I brought little from Carina. A clean shirt I was now wearing and a pair of shorts. Both of our passports were in my pocket, so other than that the only thing left was just the clothes we bought yesterday. Nothing we couldn't live without.

I counted two, but it was a safe bet there were a few more.

If I warned Allie, she might not be able to resist looking. Best to wait until I needed her to react.

After smearing a glob of guava jelly over my toast, I took a bite. Just because someone is planning to kill me doesn't mean I shouldn't enjoy my breakfast. There was a good chance it would be a while before we could eat again. Eat when you can. It was an important rule in Afghanistan, and I tried to follow it.

"I'm stuffed," Allie muttered, pushing her plate away.

"Good," I replied, pulling $50 from my pocket. I wasn't sure how much the meal was, but I didn't want to skip out on the waitress.

"What's wrong?" Allie questioned.

"Keep your eyes on me," I ordered. "Smile."

She obeyed.

"We are being watched. Don't look."

She blinked as the smile faded.

"Keep smiling," I urged, and her face immediately lit up.

Below, a woman and man pulled up on a scooter. A rental that costs a hundred bucks a day. The couple was talking, taking their time.

"Follow me closely," I told her.

The fifty slipped under the coffee cup as I stood up. My hand pressed against the small of Allie's back, guiding her toward the stairs.

"Step behind me," I urged her before we descended the steps.

She obeyed, taking a backward step as I moved in front of her. The first man lifted his head slightly as we stepped onto the sidewalk. He made a motion I could only catch in the corner of my eye. A signal.

The couple on the scooters was speaking French.

"Sorry," I blurted out, shoving the man back and grabbing the key in the woman's hand.

"*Au secours. Arrête-le,*" she screamed.

My leg swung over the seat as I started the scooter. The man across the street realized what was happening. He pushed off the wall and ran toward the street.

"Get on!" I ordered Allie.

I spotted three other men moving from the shadows to intercept us. As soon as Allie's hand grabbed my side, I throttled the scooter, whipping into the throng of traffic. The men were motioning in the rearview mirror.

Several started running down the sidewalk after us. Two jumped into a small hatchback that was attempting to maneuver down the street.

The tires of the scooter bounded over a curb as I steered past a line of vendors.

I glanced ahead to see the wall of tourists coming off the docks. The already clogged streets were about to get busier.

The hatchback jumped the curb, sending pedestrians and peddlers scurrying away. They plowed through racks of t-shirts and tables covered in compact discs.

I whipped the handlebars to the right, zipping between a small truck and cab. The tires skidded to a stop leaving a black mark on the white sidewalk, and my right foot caught the ground before I twisted the throttle and weaved through the street.

The hatchback screeched as it bounced off the truck and plowed through a wooden cart. The two men on foot were running up past the splintered cart. One pulled a gun up and fired into the crowd. The crowd erupted in screams of terror, scattering in a million directions.

13

As a general rule, individuals act similar when faced with the same situation. Put those same people in a group, and the collective reacts in wildly different patterns. A single person would seek cover during an active shooting. A crowd of tourists, though, scatters around like billiard balls, only there are hundreds of them.

The first gunshot is a surprise. If the individual recognizes the sound, the reaction might be to . However, a gunshot rarely sounds like a gunshot. On a crowded street filled with honking horns, screaming children, and squawking vendors, the bang is muted–a popping noise. Only the closest to the gunman get the reverberating blast. Those are the first to react, scattering like a tight triangle of colorful balls.

The rest of the throng might have heard the pop, but the brain never defined it for them. Their reaction is to the screaming panic coming from the pack. Fear grabs hold. Everyone reacts differently.

The crowded sidewalks poured people into the streets. Mothers scooped up kids while strangers plowed over each other.

I saw the first shot in the rearview mirror as I leaned forward in a futile attempt to boost our speed. The cartel gunman was too far away to be exact. He fired three times in our direction. Accurate or not, those rounds had to go somewhere. I didn't want the man to get a lucky shot. More than one death occurred by pure luck.

The scattering throng of people provided a lot of cover, but the Soria Cartel didn't care who they killed while trying to kill Allie. The only way to prevent more death was to remove the target from the field.

Wrenching the handlebars left, I whipped through the chaos. The sidewalk had cleared, leaving only a few smart folks hiding behind a barrier. The scooter slid across the concrete and slammed into a column. The rough edge scraped my leg as I throttled down.

"The car!" Allie shouted in my ear.

The hatchback was barreling toward us, having squeezed between two abandoned cars. Three seconds later, we would have been smashed between the hood and the post. Instead, I raced down the path.

A small market was ahead on the left. We had walked through it yesterday. There were a flight of narrow steps leading down to a galleria of shops. My hand squeezed the brake as my left foot stepped down on the sidewalk. The scooter turned, pivoting with my leg as I gunned the motor.

As I reached the top of the staircase, I released the throttle and yelled, "Hang on!"

The brakes engaged as we began a bumpy descent. Allie screamed as her grip tightened around my waist. As long as we didn't get thrown off we might make it.

The stairwell seemed too narrow for the car, and I hoped they weren't stupid enough to try. If it did fit through the opening, it would be like a boulder chasing us through a cave.

No time to focus on them. It took all my arm strength to hold the scooter straight as we bounced down each step. The wheels were too small, and each drop screeched with a grinding crunch as the fender smashed and scraped across the steps.

When we reached the bottom, I sighed with relief. The men from the car jumped out and ran down the stairs after us. The scooter's motor revved as I drove through the corridor, passing shops laden with t-shirts, baskets, and hand-carved trinkets.

The hall emptied out the back of the building onto a tiny pothole-filled drive winding past the rear of the galleria intended for deliveries. A small box truck blocked the drive, and we squeezed past the vehicle by pulling our legs up and gouging the red finish on the little bike.

By the time we got around the vehicle, three men dashed out of the tunnel behind us. The truck provided cover as they fired in our direction. The scooter screamed as we fled the scene.

A minute later, the scooter rounded the next building into a tiny parking lot. My fingers tightened around the brake, skidding the scooter to a stop.

"Off!" I ordered as I swung my leg over. We sprinted into a three-story office building next to the lot.

A flight of wooden stairs in the atrium led up to a Tarot reader. A balcony skirted the top floor and at the end of the walkway, we found ourselves overlooking a small pizza shop. The roof was mostly flat with a gabled peak that resembled the point of a hat resting on the pizza place.

"Can you jump it?" I asked, pointing at the ten foot drop to the roof of the neighboring building.

Allie nodded.

"Follow me," I urged. I bounded over the railing and dropped. My legs bent as I landed on the roof.

Allie wasted no time, and I caught her as she landed.

"Come on," I demanded, pulling her along the roof until we crossed a five-foot gap to the next building. We cowered behind a gable and waited.

In the distance, I heard sirens approaching. The local police would be looking for the two tourists that stole a scooter. There were hundreds of people on the street who might describe us. The scooter would be easy to trace to the woman we stole it from.

Hopefully, the constabulary would be more earnest in searching for the gunmen. By now, they had gone to ground, but the island isn't that big.

Allie huffed as she tried to catch her breath.

"What are we going to do, Chase?" she muttered after a few minutes.

"Wait. We need to get out of the city."

"How did they find us?" she asked.

It was the same question I had when I first saw them. Now that I had a moment to think about it, I considered a couple of things.

"From Swan Island, there were only a few places that were direct routes. Jamaica makes sense," I explained. "Of course, the passport seems likely. Just because they came to Jamaica, there was no way to pinpoint us that quick. Someone tipped them off."

"Who is doing this to me?" Allie moaned.

My arm wrapped around her, and I pulled her closer. There wasn't a lot of solace, much less answers, I could offer.

We didn't do anything wrong. Except steal a scooter. In America, a good lawyer would get that tossed out of court. We were fleeing for our lives. In Jamaica, the rules weren't always the same. If we were arrested, the police would separate us. It wasn't unfeasible to think the Sorias capable of walking into the jail and shooting us in our cells. It wouldn't matter if they bribed the guards or killed them. We'd be dead all the same.

No, the best option was to avoid the law enforcement. If they didn't arrest us, there were still too many questions to answer. Answers took time. Time was all the Sorias needed to find us.

When I was a boy, I would go hunting with my grandfather. "Patience is the key," he would say. If we waited long enough and stayed quiet, a deer would cross our path eventually. He often reminded me that whether it was the hunter or the hunted, the patient one would win the day.

Right now, I felt like the prey. How long do we wait before moving? The biggest obstacle was our location. We were invisible to anyone on the street, but we were on a tar roof in the midday sun. No water. No shelter. We'd start to bake soon.

Allie had the fairer skin. Mine had endured enough rays to turn a dark tan. I stripped my shirt off and wrapped it over Allie's head.

"Keep it covered," I warned her.

"What about you?" she asked.

"Hopefully by the time I need it, we'll be on the ground."

The black roof was already too hot to touch. I guessed it was at least 130 degrees. Heat waves emanated all around us. I crawled up the roof, using the tips of my fingers. The skin burned on the sizzling roof.

I peered over the gable. The streets were blocked by two police cars. Officers were milling around the sidewalks. I dropped below the ridge. We'd be waiting for a few minutes.

"You think Steven has a connection to the Canadian government?" I asked Allie when I settled back down beside her.

"Yeah, we've got contacts all throughout the country."

I thought for a second. "I bet it's not uncommon for an employee to need to get a passport overseas. That many ships running around the globe. Plenty of people lose their identification."

Allie mused, "I've never thought about it."

"It makes sense. A company as big as Banyan Freight must have someone that deals with that sort of thing. They would want to smooth out the bureaucracy as much as they could."

"I've been thinking about something," Allie commented. "Dad made a comment before heading to Panama. Something along the line of finding a box. We often refer to shipping containers as 'boxes.' I figured it was innocuous. Customers always hound us about their freight. It could have been anything."

"Kinda unusual for the CEO to go do inventory," I remarked.

"Not Dad. He's always hands-on. If he doesn't...didn't get the answer he wanted or thought was right, he'd go find it himself."

She continued, "If someone was smuggling drugs through our company, it would be damned near impossible to do so without some record. Not for any real quantity."

"I'd presume that if the Soria Cartel killed him over it, it had to be a significant amount," I pointed out, wiping the sweat from my forehead.

"Dad wouldn't do it," she insisted. "I know that."

"But maybe he found out about it somehow," I added.

"Right," she agreed.

"Let's play devil's advocate," I began. "If you were going to smuggle a lot of drugs, how would you do it?"

Allie explained, "I've been learning about how the company works. I might not get all the details correct, but I can give you a gist."

She continued, "Every ship has a manifest. It's fairly detailed, to a point. Usually it's just a list of shipping container numbers with the location on the ship. There will be a point of shipment and point of receiving. The manifest might have a brief description of what's inside the container, but it's not usually detailed. It might say equipment, botanicals, etc."

"Botanicals?" I questioned.

"Anything grown and harvested," Allie told me. "Like spices or vegetables."

"How do you know that's what's in there?"

"It's declared by the shipper," she explained. "We can't check, because most containers are sealed. When a manufacturer or whatever loads their container, they seal it. Technically, the only people besides the receiver that can break the seal is a government agent, like customs."

I nodded. "I could fill a container with marijuana and tell you it's rubber balls?"

"Technically, yes," she affirmed. "But there are still inspections. Customs can randomly open and verify the contents of any container. Most ports have drug-sniffing dogs too."

"You think the dogs would find every one that has drugs?"

Allie shrugged. "I can't say. Obviously drugs are smuggled in some way, but we'd at least have a paper trail."

We waited in the heat. My skin began to heat up as the sun baked me. After another half an hour, I scampered to the top of the roof. A police presence still moved about the avenue, but pedestrian traffic had started again.

I watched a few more minutes as two more patrol cars left the scene. The timer in my head told me we'd been up here a little over an hour. We needed to get down, find some water, and figure out what we were going to do.

"I need to go back to Panama," Allie blurted out.

I glanced over at her.

"Someone killed my father there. They tried to kill me too. Whatever it was, Dad must have found it there. Or, at least, he was looking for it there."

"We have to assume they are watching my boat. The airport too."

"Could we get to Kingston?" she asked. "Catch a plane out of there?"

"I'm worried that no matter what we do, we'll send up a flag to someone. They might have someone waiting to pick us off at the airport in Panama."

Allie grunted with frustration.

"Let's get down from here," I suggested. "I have an idea."

Allie returned my shirt, and we crawled across the roof to the far side. The next building was only a single story with a six-foot gap between where we stood and the next roof. The plus side was the roof had a steep gable which slanted almost to the ground.

The downside was trying to stick a landing on a surface that was angled at 135 degrees.

I took the first jump, landing in a rolling crouch. My torso twisted, and I slid down the roof about ten feet before I stopped my momentum.

My feet braced myself so I could catch Allie. She leaped. Her landing was awkward, and she rolled faster than I had. My hands slowed her, but the impact bowled me off my feet. Gravity took over from there, and I slid on my ass toward the edge.

My body turned as my feet dropped over the edge. My arms caught the gutter, and I found myself dangling about ten feet above the ground. I hung for a second to ensure I wasn't about to drop on anything that might damage me.

Once I saw it was clear, I released my grip and landed on my feet.

"Chase?" Allie called from above.

"I'm good," I responded. "Just ease your way to the edge."

She dropped into my arms, and I set her down on the asphalt.

"Now what?" she asked.

"Let's get a drink."

14

The road was nothing but dirt and what might have been gravel two decades ago. Towering juniper cedars filtered the sunlight. Gashes tore through the path from heavy rains, leaving trenches up to a foot deep in certain areas.

Small lush bushes dotted with beautiful pink flowers took over the roadside. If I stared straight at the blossom, the yellow round center seemed to stare back at me.

The four-wheel-drive Toyota truck jerked and bounced over the road.

"The coast is nice, but it's hard to beat the beauty of the backcountry," Jagger explained to Allie as if he were giving her the tour.

"What are those flowers?" she asked, pointing at the bushes.

"That, sweetheart, is the Jamaican Rose. The forest is covered with them. Mostly on the edges though."

"It's beautiful."

"Locals make a tea out of it," he told her. "It's best with a dollop of honey, but Kimmie will often put it over ice."

When we dropped off the top of the building, we needed to stay out of sight of the constabulary and the cartel. While we were being pursued, I counted at least six men chasing us. Those guys could have been anywhere.

I led Allie back to The Pelican Grill, where I left a message for Lewis Jagger with Milly.

"What makes you think he'll come?" Allie asked as we waited in the graveyard.

"Because I asked," I explained. "He'll do it because I'm a Marine, and he's a Marine."

She shook her head. "I guess I don't get it. It's not like you served together."

"I'm sure it's a trait between all the branches, but there is a pride that comes from becoming a Marine. We have each other's backs. I'd die for any of the guys in my unit. Really, they are still an extension of myself. Other Marines are like immediate family. It doesn't matter what they do."

Allie seemed to accept my answer, if she understood it or not. She leaned against a post and stared across the Old Jewish Cemetery.

The graveyard was an ideal rendezvous. A 20-minute hike away from Gloucester Avenue made it a quiet retreat. A weathered plaque declared it one of the oldest on the island, established in the 1600s. Time had not been kind, and the grounds were in some disrepair. The grass was almost to my knees. Weather-worn tombstones littered the graveyard. Some broken in several pieces.

At five minutes till three, an old black Toyota 4Runner parked on the street. Lewis Jagger climbed out of the cab.

"Told ya," I gloated.

We needed to get off the island. When I remembered the conversation with Lewis Jagger the night before, his friend, the Marine pilot and smuggler, might be our best bet.

"I imagine he'll take you," Jagger replied once we climbed into the cab of his truck. "But Viener likes his money. I wouldn't trust him too far."

Allie interjected, "I thought all Marines stick together."

Jagger chuckled. "Oh, we do. Just some of us have fewer scruples than others."

"So, he'll take us, but it's going to cost?" she asked.

"If Viener realizes how desperate you are, it will cost more," Jagger responded.

"Then we don't act desperate," she commented.

Jagger bellowed in laughter. "Sweetheart, you're looking to sneak out of the country on an unregistered flight. You're the poster child for desperate."

"We don't have any money," she told him.

"No," I responded. "We're going to have to come to an arrangement. We pay him when we get to Panama. Assuming you can get your hands on cash there."

"That'll cost you more," Jagger quipped.

The drive was a little over four hours. Most of the roads we traveled were paved highways, barely wide enough for two vehicles to pass but paved nonetheless. The last hour had been pitching over holes and ruts along the jungle road. The last signs of life had been 35 minutes ago when we passed a small farm carved out of the trees. In the corner of the ten acres of crops stood a metal shed. A single blade plow was resting against a tree. From a makeshift corral built from wooden pallets, an old worn donkey watched the truck amble past.

Allie stared out the left window. I wondered what she was thinking. Complacency took only a day to creep over us. Her thoughts must have been harried. It wasn't something I was going to bring up with her now.

"What's that?" she exclaimed from the back.

Jagger slammed on his brakes and dropped the Toyota into neutral. "Damned mongoose," he hissed as he climbed out of the cab. He pulled an old Remington .22 rifle from the storage box in the bed.

"What's he doing?" Allie asked.

The .22 cracked, sending an echo into the trees. Jagger's hand jerked the lever down, loading another round into the chamber. A second report resounded through the jungle. Jagger stomped across the dirt road.

He fired a third round point blank into the animal. He traipsed back and replaced the rifle in the back of the truck.

"Why did you do that?" Allie demanded.

"Sorry, sweetheart. Those damned things kill everything. Some dumbass 150 years ago brought the damned things in to kill the rats, which they did, along with every bird, snake, lizard, and small animal on the island."

"Still..." she whispered.

If Jagger heard her, he made no sign. Instead, he shifted into first gear and plowed on ahead.

After a quarter of an hour, we reached a fork in the road. Jagger cut the wheel right, and the road started down the mountain at a steep decline. Allie let out a barely audible squeal as the truck picked up speed. Jagger pressed his foot against the brake for the next mile as he tried to keep the truck bouncing along at a manageable speed.

At the bottom of the hill, the road flattened for a quarter mile before it began the treacherous climb. The road wasn't designed by any engineer who would keep the incline minimal by rounding the mountain with the trail. No, this was a straight shot toward the peak.

My head pressed against the seat as I watched the top of the road. Like the beginning of a rollercoaster, the only thing visible was where the dirt path vanished into the sky. What happened once we crested it was going to be a surprise.

Jagger kept the accelerator to the floor, but the truck was only in second gear. The engine whined, begging us to stop our ascent. Each jolt as the tires bounced through the ruts felt like I might tumble over backward. I ground my teeth, thinking this might be worse than the downhill trek we'd just completed.

As the hood of the Toyota climbed over the peak, it relieved me to see the road level out on top of this plateau.

"Hallelujah!" Allie praised as she saw the flat stretch ahead.

"That was a nail-biter, wasn't it?" Jagger joked. "I haven't been that straight up since my 50s."

Allie relaxed as well with a long sigh, as if she released a breath she held in her lungs for hours.

"The airfield is right up here," Jagger commented. "I think."

"You ever been up here?" I asked.

"Nah," he replied. "Now that I've been, I have little use to go up that hill again."

"Me neither," Allie gasped.

"Sweetheart, don't forget if we leave it's back down that monstrosity."

"Hell, I'll walk," she snapped.

"With any luck," I told her, "we'll be flying out."

Jagger glanced back at Allie with a sly grin, saying, "If he's home."

Allie groaned. Jagger had a point. He knew where Viener was, but there was no way to call him. We knew that going into it. Whatever the outcome, we needed to get out of Montego Bay if we wanted to leave the country unnoticed.

The top of this mountain looked like it had been shaved clean of trees. Ahead, a strip of dirt stretched a half a mile to a big metal barn operating as a hangar. The doors were open, and the nose of an old gray plane peeked out like a prairie dog.

A fuel tank stood about 12 feet in the air. I wondered how a fuel truck could make it up the hill to refill the thing.

A black SUV was parked next to the building. It was the only thing near the building not covered in rust.

Jagger braked. "I don't want to rush up on the man," he advised. "Fool's likely to shoot first before we can make any introductions."

A tall black man appeared in the hangar's doorway. He was wearing a suit, which seemed out of place here.

"He has a big knife!" Allie exclaimed.

I took another look to see a second man show up, holding what might have been a machete.

"Damn," Jagger muttered, throwing the Toyota into reverse.

"Do those guys look official to you?" I asked the old Marine as he backed out of their line of sight.

"Official trouble."

"Could they be with the cartel?" Allie asked. Her voice trembled.

"I don't see how," I responded.

"Mexican cartels hold little weight around here," Jagger told us. "We got the Shower Posse, and they aren't gonna let any Mexicans interfere with their business. I imagine those fellows are Posse. If Viener is running drugs, he's doing it for them."

"Maybe we should back up before they see us," I pointed out.

"You think your friend is in trouble?" Allie asked as Jagger parked the Toyota behind a copse of trees.

"It could just be a regular business thing," Jagger commented.

He and I exchanged glances. The situation was complicated. That sense of duty I told Allie about was real. If Viener was in trouble, we needed to step in and help. But, if the situation was simply a transaction, we might make things worse.

"How good are you with that rifle?" I asked.

"I mean, it's a .22. I can hit anything you want me to hit, but I can't guarantee it's going to go down."

The .22 was a small round. Even up close, it took three shots to kill the mongoose. It can be deadly, but from this distance, the shooter had to hit the right part of the human body to kill it. There has been more than one instance where a person has taken a .22 bullet and continued as if it were just a bee sting.

"It's the best we got, I guess," I told him.

The plan was simple. Jagger sets himself up with the rifle while I approach. This was mostly reconnaissance: investigate and see if Viener was in trouble. Of course, even if it were just routine business, I'd be walking into the midst of an illicit deal. Viener might not be in trouble, but it would put a bullseye on me.

"I can go too," Allie suggested.

"Oh, no," I told her. "You stay here with Lewis. If something goes wrong, get in the truck and hightail it down that mountain."

"Chase!" she protested. "They may not shoot you if there's a woman with you."

"Sweetheart," Jagger interrupted. "Those boys would shoot their sister if she screwed with their money."

Allie huffed, and I looked at Jagger. "Anything goes wrong, get her out of here."

"You got it," he vowed.

The two men had stepped back into the hangar. I marched in double-time toward the building. I was still wearing shorts and sandals, looking every bit the part of a beach bum.

The trick was to sneak up on the building without looking like I was sneaking up on the building. If it looked like I belonged, the men inside might not react too violently. If they saw me crouching and hiding, suspicions would flare along with whatever weapons they carried.

When I reached the building, I heard groaning. It's an easily recognizable noise. The sound of someone suffering. Whether or not that someone was Viener, this no longer felt like the type of business deal I would want to find myself in.

If I entered the building, Jagger didn't have a shot. That meant I needed to bring them outside.

"This is your last fucking chance!" a voice shouted in a thick Jamaican accent. "Where is my cocaine, Eric?"

Definitely not a business deal.

I picked up a rock and threw it against a metal drum. The gong echoed off the metal sides of the barn. Three black men barreled out of the hangar. The tall man wearing the suit stood in the center. The other two men flanked him, one carried a machete while the other held a wooden Louisville Slugger. The bat was stained brown with some fresh blood caked to the end.

15

"Da 'ell!" the man in the suit exclaimed.

"Sorry, man," I apologized, lifting my palms up in feigned contrition. "I had some car trouble. My wife and I have been exploring the mountains in our four-by-four. Seems like we hit something. Oil's everywhere. The engine's smoking."

As I rambled, I moved toward them casually. Just a dumb American who can't handle the wilds of Jamaica.

"This is the only place around," I continued. "Just hoping to find some help."

The man holding the machete leered at me before mumbling something to Suit. Slugger found me amusing, chuckling at the dumb American.

"No 'un kin hep you he'e," Suit told me.

"Doesn't one of you have a phone?" I pleaded, taking a step toward Slugger. He was the least on-guard, still finding me amusing.

"Dere's no service he'e," Suit replied. "Git outta he'e, or else."

I wondered if they just didn't care what I saw, or if there wasn't any actual intention of letting me go. It's not that I harbor any qualms about striking first. I'm a firm believer in hit first and hit hard. For whatever reason, they did not engage me.

"Look." I was only three feet from Slugger. "Do any of you know where I can find a phone?"

"Dere's no phone!" Suit blurted out, annoyed.

"Isn't Eric here?" I asked.

The mention of Viener's name sparked something in Suit's eyes. I stepped forward with my right leg, driving my right fist into Slugger's throat. The blow carried enough force to render him gasping for air. His free hand instinctively grabbed his neck. My left hand caught the bat as my other fist chopped down on his wrist. His grip released, and I swung the wooden club in a tight arc as I dropped to my left knee.

The thick end of the bat missed Machete's kneecaps. He started his charge when my knuckles hit Slugger and my aim was a little high. The bat hit just above his knee. The meaty part of his thigh protected the bone, and while it hurt him enough that he stumbled away, there was no permanent damage.

It didn't even slow the brute who outweighed me by at least 60 pounds. Machete raised the blade to bring it down on me. With one knee in the dust, I could only roll away as the silver machete barely missed.

My right hand pushed me off the ground, and I rose to my feet with two hands clutching the bat. Slugger straightened despite the labored breathing. Unarmed, he waited to let Machete chop me up.

Machete didn't pause, charging with the blade whipping toward me. The metal edge of the blade connected with the wooden bat. The impact tore a tiny nick in the bat's surface and deflected the machete away. My left foot stepped behind my right as I drove the knob into Machete's face. The crunch of bone sounded as he grunted in pain. I twisted around, bringing my right leg completely around. The barrel of the bat ripped through the air before striking Slugger in the side of his head. The Jamaican thug crumpled to the dirt like a sheet.

I didn't hear the gunshot when Jagger fired the rifle, but as my foot planted and my arms finished following through with the swing, I saw Suit jerk as the .22 round hit his shoulder. The 9 mm he was pulling from a holster under his jacket fell to the ground. I took two quick steps forward and kicked it away from him.

"Do ya know who da fook I am?" Suit snapped.

The end cap of the bat extended toward Suit as I bent to scoop up the 9 mm. Blood smeared across Machete's stunned face as he held his hand against it.

"No, I don't," I responded. "But I don't care."

Suit scowled. He was obviously of some importance, at least to himself. The suit he wore wasn't some off-the-rack varietal. I doubted he bought it on the island. He bought that in New York or London, not Kingston. The black Land Rover parked next to the hangar was new, too. Most of the cars I'd seen in Jamaica were older, even the more luxurious ones. Suit probably imported this one especially for himself.

That kind of excess in style meant he had means. It didn't take a rocket scientist to guess that income was from drugs.

"Wut do ya wunt?" he asked.

"You can get in your truck and drive your men to the nearest hospital," I suggested.

"I'll make you pay fo dis?"

"Get in line," I told him. "Now, get out of here."

"Khenon," Suit addressed Machete. "Get Charles."

Khenon, AKA Machete, stumbled toward Slugger. "He's dead," he informed Suit.

Suit glared at me with hatred in his eyes. "Leave 'im," he demanded.

The tall black man marched to the driver's side of the Land Rover while Khenon climbed into the passenger seat. At this point, I didn't want to stay on the island too long. Suit would not take the attack kindly, and he struck me as the type that came back with a vengeance.

The SUV drove out behind the shed toward an unseen road. When the trees swallowed the sound of the Land Rover's engine, I walked inside the metal building.

A figure sat in a rolling desk chair. Blood covered his misshapen face, and his left arm was bent at an awkward angle.

"Viener?" I asked aloud, still holding the 9 mm aloft.

The man grunted something unintelligible.

"You with me?" I inquired again.

"Who are you?" he gurgled.

"Just a fellow Marine," I told him as I circled the chair.

Suit or, more likely, his men secured Viener to the armrests with electrical wire. I unwound it, freeing the man's arms.

He howled in pain when the broken arm swung free.

"Hang tight, man," I warned him. "We have to set that fracture."

An engine sounded outside. I raised the 9 mm in case it was Suit returning. Instead, Jagger's Toyota stopped in front of the open door.

"Holy shit," Jagger muttered when he saw Viener. "Those boys worked you over."

"Lewis?" Viener asked, dumbfounded.

"Yeah, boy. Looks like we got here just in time."

Allie gasped as she entered the hangar.

"We need to set his arm," I announced. "Lewis, find me something to act as a splint. Allie, look in that tool box over there for any kind of tape. Duct or electric will work best."

The two went off in opposite directions, as I leaned over Viener, looking for more serious injuries.

"What day is it?" I asked the pilot.

"Tuesday."

"Your name?" I questioned.

"Eric Kareem Viener."

"Kareem?"

"My dad was a Laker's fan," he mumbled through a swollen lip.

"Here ya go," Jagger stated, offering two slats from a wooden pallet. "Who was that, Eric?"

Viener spat a clotted clump of blood from his mouth onto the dirt floor. "Dominick Estes. He's Posse."

"Damn, son," Jagger whistled. "What'd you do to piss him off?"

Viener glanced at me with unspoken questions. Jagger nodded, saying, "He's good. Former Recon."

The battered pilot released a relieved breath once Jagger offered his appraisal of my character. "Dominick thinks I stole from a shipment of cocaine I flew up to Canada a couple of weeks ago."

"Did you?" I asked.

Viener grinned. "Of course I did. Not as much as he thinks, though," he explained. "I never take enough to be noticed."

Allie appeared at my shoulder, extending her hand with a roll of black duct tape in it. "Will this work?" she asked.

"Perfect," I acknowledged, taking the roll from her. "Lewis, break those slats down to about ten inches. Make sure the ends aren't too jagged. Do you have a first aid kit, Eric?"

"In the cockpit," he replied. I looked at Allie silently. She nodded and climbed into the plane.

"Is that a Beechcraft?" I asked as I ripped the sleeves off his shirt.

"A '56," he reported proudly.

"How often do you pilfer the cargo?" I queried as I took the two pieces of wood from Jagger.

"Every time," he admitted. "Man's got to have a retirement plan."

"You won't need a big nest egg if you rip off drug cartels," I pointed out.

"Seriously, I never take enough for them to notice."

"And yet?" Jagger noted.

"Someone down the line stole it. I just caught the blame."

"The Posse will kill you," Jagger told him.

"Yeah, it seems like my time has come."

"You ready?" I asked.

Viener nodded, and I pulled the man's wrist toward the floor. He howled in agony as the broken bones snapped back together. Jagger held the two slats on his forearm as I bound them tightly with the tape. After the wood was covered in black adhesive, I ripped the roll. The splint was as good as any cast, and as long as the pieces matched properly, Viener would heal.

"I got it," Allie shouted as she climbed out of the plane.

"Lewis, can you make sure we don't have any company coming back?" I asked.

The old Marine nodded before heading outside to his truck.

Allie took several alcohol pads from the first aid kit and started cleaning Viener's wounds. He had several gashes and bruises from the beating he received, but it looked like the arm was the first move toward a slow, torturous death.

"Thank you," Viener uttered finally.

"Well, I hope your gratitude extends to helping us next," I replied.

"Where do you want to go?" he asked, noting the only obvious help a pilot can offer is a plane ride.

"Panama."

Viener's eyes turned up toward the roof of the hangar as he made some mental calculations.

"I don't know if I can fly that far like this," he remarked.

"If you can take off and land, I can do the rest," I told him.

"You can fly?" he asked.

"I can not crash. So long as we have plenty of fuel and the weather is clear, I can hold the stick straight."

"Honey," Viener addressed Allie. "If you'll go look in that locker over there, you'll find a bottle of Vicodin and some rum. I'm gonna need both."

"You're going to fly drunk?" she asked incredulously.

"It's better than passing out in pain in the middle of takeoff."

Her face contorted with concern as she stalked toward the lockers.

"She's already been in one plane crash this week," I told Viener.

"Oh, shit," he mumbled. "There's nothing to worry about. I just don't want my arm to give out before I level off."

I nodded. "How long before Dominick can get reinforcements and return?" I asked.

"It'll take an hour and a half to get to Kingston," Viener explained. "But he'll have a phone signal in about 45 minutes."

"We have two hours," I estimated. "Shouldn't be sooner but could be later."

Viener agreed.

"How soon can you take off?" I asked.

"Let your girl bring me those pills, and you refuel the plane. We can be out of here in no less than an hour. I need to load a few things. I don't think I'll be coming back to Jamaica."

Allie returned carrying a white bottle of pills and a half-empty liter of dark rum. She opened the pill bottle and gave him two. He swallowed them with a gulp of alcohol and a resounding sigh.

"What's your name, fellow Marine?" he asked me.

"Chase. This is Allie."

"Chase, the fuel is in the big tank outside. There's an extra hose out back. The electric pump is out, so you'll need to find the manual one. I hope your arm is up for it."

"I can manage," I assured him.

"Good." He turned to Allie. "You're going to help me."

He upended the bottle and swallowed more rum.

"Should you be drinking that much?" she asked.

"I promise you; I fly drunk all the time. I've never been in a crash."

She shook her head, saying, "Until this week, neither have I."

"Well, your pilot wasn't a Marine," he remarked. "We don't crash."

It took an hour to fuel the Beechcraft. Viener had two hoses that ran from the tank outside into the hangar. The fuel pump he used was a crank model that attaches between two hoses. It took almost 20 minutes of turning the handle before I pulled enough fuel to flow through the two hoses. My arms are used to cranking winch handles to raise and lower sails, but those tasks only take two to three minutes. After an hour, my arm felt like jelly.

"Sorry, I normally pull the girl over to the pump," Viener explained. "I don't think I can handle it right now."

I didn't complain. We hadn't discussed payment for the trip yet, and while I might have prevented further torture for the pilot, my interaction with Dominick Estes didn't leave him a way out. Estes would be back to kill all of us. No doubt about that.

So, I keep cranking, while Viener continues drinking. Allie's concerns were becoming mine too, but it was best not to share that yet.

After he imbibed the majority of the bottle of rum, the man began loading boxes slowly onto a two-wheel dolly from some unseen location and loaded them into the back of the Beechcraft. Jagger maintained a watch. If he fired the .22 twice, we had company.

"She looks full," Viener commented after putting another stack of boxes in the plane. "You can help me carry some things."

He led me through a double door where the floor no longer existed. Two sheets of plywood leaned against opposite walls. He'd built a makeshift bunker. An engine had been pushed to the corner. Simple and effective. Dig a hole, hide the goodies, cover with plywood and dirt, and finally load the floor down with things that look too heavy to move.

"I can't get these boxes with one arm," he informed me.

When I dropped into the hole, I found long metal crates stacked four high. Stamped in black ink on the metal exterior were the words, "Property of the United States Marine Corps."

"What do you have here?" I asked.

"My retirement."

A low groan came from my chest. Jagger called it earlier. Some of us don't have the best scruples. Viener wasn't the first grunt to steal from the Corps. He won't be the last. I could pass judgment on him, but right now, I needed him to get us off the island.

With both arms, I hoisted the boxes out of the hole one at a time. Viener drug them over to a cart with his good hand before offering it to me as I climbed out of the hole.

Two pops resounded outside.

"Chase!" Allie shouted.

"Damn!" Viener cursed, grabbing the cart with his good arm and pushing it back into the hangar.

"Can we leave?" I asked.

"Don't got much choice."

I sprinted ahead.

"Allie, help Viener get aboard," I ordered as I ran past the plane.

Jagger was standing on the cab of his truck, pointing at a dust cloud rolling up the back of the mountain. The cars weren't visible, but with that much dust, it had to be more than just the Land Rover.

"Lewis, get out of here," I ordered. "You can get down the mountain before they make it up here."

"Will you guys make it?" he asked as the Beechcraft's engine rumbled to life.

"If we don't, neither will they," I told him.

"Oohrah!" he grunted.

My hand clasped his shoulder in gratitude.

"When you come back for your boat, we are getting drunk," he warned me.

"I'm game."

He tossed me the .22 as he climbed down. "Keep it. You might need it before you get off the ground."

I nodded in appreciation.

"Be careful," I advised. "Don't stop until you get to MoBay."

"Hell, son, I already gotta pee," he joked as he slammed the driver's door.

The Toyota bounced across the field toward the dirt path we drove coming up the mountain. The journey down this rock wasn't one I envied, but it might be better than what was coming up the other side.

"Yo!" Viener yelled. "You coming?"

With the rifle in my hand, I jogged toward the gangway. Viener was already climbing aboard with the wheel chocks slung over his shoulder when I got there. Before I was up the ladder, the aircraft moved forward.

The door was still open, and I crouched beside it with the .22 ready to aim. The dust cloud was almost on us as the tail cleared the hangar.

"Everyone hang on to something," Viener announced.

Allie strapped into a jump seat behind me.

"Chase?" she blurted.

"Give me a minute," I retorted, focusing my sights on the hood of an old Bronco cresting the hill.

Viener didn't waste time, and the Beechcraft picked up speed.

A black man leaned out the passenger's window with what looked like an Uzi. The metal skin of the craft pinged as a blast of bullets hit us. I lined up the iron sights with the man's head and squeezed the trigger. My aim was too far to the left, but I winged him in the arm. He would not be able to use that arm to fire another burst from the Uzi just yet.

With the gunner out of commission for a second, the driver of the Bronco gunned the engine, determined to outrace the Beechcraft. Two other vehicles emerged from the cloud of dust. The Land Rover and an older Jeep Cherokee.

The Bronco was gaining on us, but as long as he didn't get too close, we should have no trouble taking off. I retrained my sights on the front of the Bronco. The .22 might not do a lot of damage, but it might do enough.

My finger squeezed, and by the time the gun-shot echoed in the Beechcraft's cabin, I'd jacked another bullet into the chamber and fired.

From my vantage point it appeared both shots hit the grill of the Bronco. I hoped that they would punch a hole through the radiator. It was a Hail Mary shot, but if it worked, they'd be leaving the truck on the mountain until they found a new radiator.

The other two cars were far enough behind that they posed no danger. We were almost to takeoff speed. I pulled the cabin door closed and dropped the lever, securing it just as the wheels lifted off the ground.

My hands caught the freight straps on the side. I heaved against the inertia that wanted to throw me toward the back of the plane. As we climbed toward the sky, I strapped into the other jump seat, and breathed a sigh of relief.

Across from me, Allie's fingers were white from gripping the canvas strap over her shoulders.

16

The Banyan Freight office in Panama City took up space in a small, grungy building three blocks from the port. I wasn't expecting what I saw. I imagined the office in some high-rise.

This was my first visit to Panama. After seeing different cities across the globe, I've learned that everywhere defies my expectation. Panama City was a sprawling city with more traffic than I'd seen, even in Miami. Perhaps New York or San Francisco beat it. In any case, I didn't want to drive in it.

Viener, a consummate smuggler, knew exactly where to land the Beechcraft without the prying eyes of anyone. Unfortunately, the airstrip sat 30 miles north of the city in the middle of farmland, and it took about an hour to flag down a ride. A delivery driver took mercy on us when we explained Viener had been in an accident and needed to get to a hospital.

Just like the Swan Islands, I found it difficult to navigate without Allie's Spanish, which appeared to a Luddite like myself to be near fluent. She conversed with the driver up front while Viener and I relegated ourselves to the back of the truck. Another mental note jotted across the to-do list in my mind—learn Spanish.

"You plan on taking her back into the lion's den?" Viener asked as our heads bobbed side to side with each bump the wheels hit.

"I'm not taking her anywhere," I corrected. "I'm just tagging along."

"Seems pretty convenient you happened to be there when her plane went down," he suggested.

I shook my head. People like Viener trusted no one, partly because they weren't trustworthy. He didn't strike me as a bad guy, just one that succumbed to temptation. Despite the years he had on me, I sensed a familiarity in him. It wasn't hard to pinpoint. Tristan. A kid in my unit in Afghanistan. Hell of a fighter. Even took a bullet for me once.

But Tristan never seemed satisfied. He wanted the shortcut, and he simply made his life harder. Until he ran out of time.

I missed him, but as I talked to Viener on the flight over, I realized this might have been Tristan. If he'd survived.

Viener was where Tristan would have ended up. There'd always be someone he crossed for a few dollars that would be gunning for him.

Tristan had been a lost cause, and Viener had a good quarter of a century on my friend. This old pilot's mold had set. This was who he was. A loner. Barely scraping by. He survived on gleaning from the smuggled freight he was running. I'd guess any bit he got ahead would find its way into someone else's pocket, whether it paid for rum, pills, or women.

"What's your plan after this?" I asked him.

"I figure somewhere in Central America there's an abandoned airstrip just begging for someone to run a plane through it. I'll make do."

Since the delivery truck had no lighting in the back, we sat in complete darkness. The only illumination came from the sliver of light sneaking in around the door. He couldn't see me shake my head in disbelief. There's no point in reminding him how close he had been to being chopped into small pieces. He escaped, mostly unscathed, to fight again.

"You ever want to make some dough," he commented, "then hit me up. You got the muscle, I got the brains. We could make lots of money."

I chuckled in the dark. "I'll stick to my gig."

"Saving damsels in distress?"

My chuckle turned into a full-fledged laugh. "It doesn't pay great, but the benefits..."

The truck had slowed down over the last few minutes, and I guessed we were getting into traffic. The Panamanian sun quickly evolved this back end into a broiler, and I hoped we'd get out soon.

After fleeing Jamaica, I felt like we were in the same predicament that we had when we made landfall in Jamaica. Only this time, it wasn't just Allie with only the clothes on her back. I still had several hundred dollars in cash, but it wouldn't last long.

Allie already mentioned making a withdrawal from either the bank or whatever petty cash the Banyan Freight office had. When we walked into the office, we would become reacquired targets, so getting flush with cash now made sense.

When the truck finally stopped, Allie opened the rear to let us out in front of a small clinic.

"You should be able to get that properly tended to here," Allie informed him.

"I'll be at the plane after this. I'll wait a day or so on you."

"Thanks, Eric," Allie acknowledged.

"I have a satellite phone on the plane," he told us. "Give me a call if you need a quick getaway."

He handed me a piece of paper with a number on it. "Don't forget," he added, cutting his eyes toward Allie. "I work for tips."

He winked before turning toward the clinic.

From the clinic, Allie flagged down a taxi where we spent the next two hours crawling through the bumper-to-bumper traffic.

"Do you spend a lot of time in Panama?" I asked her.

"Dad had offices all over the globe, but with the traffic through the canal, this was his busiest port. We'd spend at least one week a month here as kids. During the school year, we'd spend most of our time in Toronto, but he came down here constantly."

As we crept along the road, I watched the people walking past. The women dressed fairly elegantly. Not a single person I saw wore shorts or a t-shirt. In fact, it took me a second to register that every woman walked around in high heels. Almost all donned dresses, with only a few outliers in pants. Even those were still what I considered dressy, but I'm still wearing sandals and the same pair of shorts from yesterday.

Mostly, the men shared the style of the women. With few exceptions that sported jerseys and shorts, most of them wore collared shirts and slacks. Like the women, I noted very few males wearing running shoes or sandals. I'm going to stick out like a sore thumb. In fact, I noticed several eyes scan me as I passed.

"I've never been so under-dressed for an entire country," I commented.

Allie gave me a quick look. "Panamanians don't dress down often. Even government buildings refuse entry if one is dressed like you are."

"Well, I guess modern beach bum hasn't made it here yet," I joked.

She gave me some side-eye with a slight groan.

Panama City seemed to invest in wiring and construction. Every road seemed to be undergoing some work, a major contribution to the traffic situation we tried to slog through. As we passed the fourth intersection, I counted a minimum of two spools of wire measuring no less than three feet in diameter each. Most seemed to feed to a pole or through pipes in the ground. It reminded me of the old telephone cables strung up in the country.

"How many people work in your office here?" I asked.

"Six total. Denise manages the office. There are a couple of Logistic Managers and three Shipyard Supervisors. They rotate between the office and the port."

The cab turned out of the heavy traffic.

Allie told the driver to stop. "We can walk from here," she advised.

She led me two blocks to the dirty gray building.

"Fancy," I remarked with a heavy dose of snark.

"Yeah, but it's also far from all the good places to eat," she retorted.

"The benefits astound."

Once we passed through the doors, the building morphed into a mid-range office, something that might befit a successful insurance representative or a decent dentist. Modest but nice. The furnishings were a notch above basic. Banyan Freight didn't use this office to woo potential customers. Its decor was modern, utilitarian like a bourbon you only offered to acquaintances.

"Ms. Tremblay?"

The questioning voice belonged to a blond woman in her 30s perched behind a desk stacked with various sized piles of papers.

"Afternoon Denise," Allie acknowledged. The office manager.

Denise's left hand had neither a gold band nor the imprint of one. Based on her voice, she was either a Midwestern American or Canadian. Did she come to Panama for the job? Or was there another reason? Perhaps it was just because she wanted to. Most people don't get out of their comfort zones, and I found it curious what brought her here.

"I'm going to be in Dad's office," Allie explained.

"Yes," Denise responded. Her face twisted with confusion as she opened a drawer to remove a key ring she handed to Allie. She had questions but didn't ask them. What was Allie doing here? Maybe she heard about the plane crash. Or she heard about it going missing.

"Also, I need the petty cash box," Allie demanded. "Include all the receipts."

I followed two steps behind Allie like an obedient dog as we passed Denise's desk. With a stolen glance, I noticed most of the papers looked like shipping documents.

How freight maneuvered around the world made little sense to me. It wasn't something I dealt with. Would every piece going through the Canal have to pass through customs? That might generate a lot of paperwork. It wasn't likely very similar to passing through various countries' custom processes. Much grander, I assumed.

The hallway behind Denise had six doors. One bore a placard reading "Restroom." Three were closed. Two doors were opened, but only one office was currently occupied by a dark-skinned man behind a desk. He didn't register us as we passed his door, instead, he seemed intently focused on a computer monitor.

At the end of the hall, the last door was locked. Allie used the keys from Denise's desk to open the door. When we entered the office, we might as well have passed through to Narnia. The stark difference between the decor was blatant.

Dark wood bookcases lined the boss's office. The shelves held an array of pottery and art that appeared to be pre-Columbian. I slowly circled the room, examining each piece. They appeared authentic, and I wondered at the legality of them.

Perhaps there was no issue if they didn't leave the country. Over the centuries, grave robbers and looters have ransacked archaeological sites for pre-Columbian art. Many countries fought back by outlawing the export. Someone like Roger Tremblay might circumvent the rules by building a collection in the country.

Some pieces seemed to be pristine, leaving me to estimate their value as priceless. Of course, on the black market, everything technically has a price.

I didn't mention it to Allie, but the mere fact that suspect artifacts decorated his office gave me pause to question his ethics. In fact, the art might have been payment for other unethical actions. It raised questions I doubted had answers.

"You like them?" she asked as I continued my journey around Tremblay's museum.

"They are beautiful," I told her.

"Dad's been a collector for years. He loaned a collection to the museum here in Panama City. His Mayan collection is on display at the capitol in Mexico City."

"Some of these are museum quality," I pointed out.

"Yeah, he has a good eye."

She sat at her father's desk. "I don't even know what to look for," she remarked.

"You mentioned he was trying to find some missing freight. How would he do that?"

She turned on his computer. While it powered up, she opened the file drawer on the desk.

Tremblay's desk was neat, unlike Denise's. Maybe Denise cleaned it up after his death. Unfortunately, Tremblay's untimely death didn't slow the freight business. Anything he was working on currently would have been out, and it would still need immediate attention despite the man's death. The show, after all, must go on. Some of those papers cluttering Denise's workspace may have once lived on this enormous oak desk.

Two knocks on the door sounded before it opened a crack. "Ms. Tremblay," Denise called, "Here is the petty cash. The receipts are in the box. It was reconciled the day Mr. Tremblay...your father was killed."

Allie nodded without making eye contact. Her hand extended to take the small lock-box from the office manager. There was a distinct disdain from both of them. The kind of attitude both would deny if asked, but it still festered under the surface. I wondered what the impetus for it was. No point in asking. Allie wouldn't acknowledge it.

"What's with the receipts?" I asked.

She shook her head. "Nothing really. Just common practice to reconcile the cash with the receipts. If she knew I was taking all of the cash, she might want to know why."

"Do you have to tell her?" I questioned. "It's your company."

"It just alleviates the worry that I might be stealing."

"But it's your company," I reiterated.

"It's a public company that my family holds majority share in. One can't take money out without a reason. That's still embezzling"

I shrugged as I leaned forward in my chair. Three picture frames angled toward Tremblay's seat. My index finger pushed the frame around until I could see the image. A woman in her 40s with blue eyes, dirty blond hair, and perfectly white teeth lined up in a beatific smile. Everything about the picture, from the slight sepia look to the woman's hairstyle, dated this image to the mid-90s.

"My mom," Allie informed me. It was an assumption I'd already made.

"She's beautiful," I noted. "I see a lot of her in you."

Allie grinned, and the smile mirrored the one frozen on her mother's face.

She returned to the drawer as the computer whirred and buzzed to life. I picked up the picture of Allie. It was several years old. Allie looked to be in college, or at least she seemed the right age.

The third picture was of another girl in a wedding dress. The woman was in her 20s. I guessed it was Sarah, Allie's sister. She had the same blue eyes as her mother, but the shape of her mouth was a little lop-sided compared to Allie and their mother.

I stared at the picture as I sat on the corner of the desk.

"How old was your sister when she got married?" I asked.

"23."

The frame felt strange. Or rather, it looked weird. The picture appeared warped. Almost as if the photograph had gotten wet and buckled.

My fingers rotated the picture frame. The cardboard backing had a little brass latch twisted to hold the opening closed. The cardboard door bulged. I opened the cardboard door, and a thickly folded wad of paper pushed the back open and dropped to the desk.

"What are you doing?" Allie asked with a mixture of annoyance and curiosity.

I unfolded the paper to find three sheets of white legal pad paper filled with numbers on every line. Allie reached over and grabbed the papers from my hand. She studied them for a second before looking up at me.

"What is it?" I asked.

"I think they are box numbers."

She used her palm to flatten the sheets next to the mouse pad. Allie turned her attention back to the screen and typed the first number into a program.

"No results," the program posted in a pop-up box.

She tried again.

"No results," it read again.

Allie navigated to a third program and input the number.

A string of numbers and words came up, followed by the words, "POL Chabahar."

"What is POL?" I asked.

"Port of Loading," Allie explained. "I don't know where Chabahar is, though. Let me pull up Google."

"Don't bother," I told her. "Chabahar is a port city in Iran."

"Oh," she commented. "It didn't show where the container is or where it was going."

"Is that unusual?"

She nodded and started typing the other numbers into the same three programs. Most had no results in any of them, but a few still showed an origin. All of them were shipping from Chabahar.

"What are they shipping from there?" she asked out loud.

"When I first went to Afghanistan, they tasked us with interrupting the flow of opium out of the Taliban's hands and into the market. The opium trade funded a lot of those cells. When we became a hindrance, the trade routes moved through Iran, where we couldn't break them up. Chabahar was a major port for that."

Allie stared up at me with bewildered eyes.

17

Two hours passed as Allie checked each number on Tremblay's list. I did not know what information Allie gleaned from the data she found. Mostly, I reclined in the high-back chair across from her. In fact, I dozed a few minutes.

Two knocks disrupted my nap.

"Ms. Tremblay?" Denise called as she cracked the door ajar.

"Yes?" Allie asked, pulling the list of numbers off the top of the desk swiftly.

"There's a call for you," she announced. "Steven's on the phone."

"Thank you," she responded.

When the door latch clicked and we were alone again, Allie's face grew concerned. She reached for the receiver as I leaned forward.

"Hello." Her voice had a slight tremble I hoped wasn't noticeable on the other end.

"Hi Steven," she responded to the caller.

"No, I'm fine," she continued.

"It's a long story."

I imagined what Steven was saying. He wanted to know what happened. Allie answered with vague phrases. She'd tell him about it later. She had no idea what happened to the plane. She was just lucky. Things like that.

Finally, she responded to a query about being in the office. Before she spoke, I watched the concern in her eyes. "I lost Daddy in the crash," she told him. The emotions filled her eyes as she continued to talk. "I guess I wanted to come back here and...I don't know exactly."

"Yes," she answered him. "I'm going to be going home soon."

Then, "I'm not sure."

The conversation continued along the same thread. The responses she offered seemed to be to innocuous questions that a family member might ask. But, if he phrased them the right way, they could be a fishing expedition. If Steven was behind it, he would have known about the attack on Swan Island and that we were in Jamaica. He just couldn't let Allie know he was aware.

"I'll call you when I decide to head home."

Finally, she said, "What does it matter? Sarah can't go, and I'm here. Anyone else can be damned. I'll arrange Daddy's memorial on my time."

She hung up after a curt good-bye.

Her woeful face lifted toward me. "He basically asked why I'm here," she told me. "Obviously, Denise called him."

"That might not be out of the ordinary," I pointed out. "It's office gossip. There would be talk about the plane crash or, at the very least, your return here so soon was a curiosity."

"He's behind it," she stated. "It was in his voice."

"If he is, we need to leave now," I told her. "He's had time to make a call. If it were me, I'd have done that before I talked to you. He just has to keep you on the line long enough for someone to get here."

A tear slid down her right cheek. Another followed. As she sat here at her father's desk, the stress and emotions that she'd avoided for the past few days swept through her. The teardrops began flowing.

"I just don't understand," she blubbered. "Why? Why would Steven do this?"

I didn't answer because I didn't have a good one. Money might be it. Although, I would think marrying into a freight baron's family offered enough money to satisfy most people. Of course, there are those that can never get enough. Steven might not be satisfied with marrying money. He needed to be his own master. Answering to the Tremblays was too much. In that case, it could be a matter of control.

Maybe it was pure hate. His wife and her family might be subject of his vitriol for no reason at all.

The motives of one individual can vary, and the variations of those thoughts are infinite.

Part of me wanted to move around the desk and comfort her. It wouldn't help. Grief, regret, and anger overcame her. A hug or a pat from me would not help. The best I could do was sit here and let her feel those emotions. The wounds bled at the moment. Soon, scabs would form, bleeding when she picked at them. When it was all said and done, the scars would remain. Reminders of the pain that no longer hurt.

Unfortunately, I didn't know how much time we had for her to live in her feelings. We'd been here long enough for someone to show up and pick us off as we left.

"Allie, we need to go," I told her as I rose to my feet.

She wiped her cheeks with her fingers until the tears smeared across her cheeks. The paper her father left was in her hand. She folded it up.

"What do we do?" she inquired.

"We have to get away from here. Preferably alone."

She rose to her feet, and I stopped her. "Don't forget your petty cash," I told her, pointing at the metal box.

Allie pulled what looked like $10,000 out of the box. The Tilly Inn has a petty cash box with about $500 for emergencies that. I wondered what Banyan Freight considered petty.

"Where are you going, Ms. Tremblay?" Denise asked urgently as we sailed through the lobby.

"Lunch," Allie lied.

"But, Ms. Tremblay," the office manager called as we pushed through the doors. The rest of her sentence was lost to the slamming door.

"That bitch called him," she mumbled.

"Given the tone of her voice, he likely wanted her to keep you there for a few minutes," I commented.

"Dammit," Allie cursed as she stormed down the sidewalk.

The approach to the building was difficult. The Banyan Freight building was the only one on the block, and the neighboring blocks consisted mostly of small service businesses, like equipment repair and maintenance offices. It felt a little like crossing through a village in Afghanistan. There were plenty of places to hide if one wanted to wait and pick off soldiers with a rifle. I felt naked, and my hand pressed against the small of Allie's back as if to hurry her along and keep her within my imaginary range of protection as I scanned the buildings for a hawk waiting on his prey.

The thing about that kind of landscape is if the predator hasn't had time to hide and await his ambush, his arrival is difficult to conceal. So, when the boxy SUV pulled onto the road a block behind us, it was obvious what was in the car–danger.

Almost every human has the built in fight-or-flight mode. Years of training equipped me to overcome the urge, allowing my brain a few seconds to decide rather than rely on my instinct. The open, empty street provided almost no cover. It was a good logical assumption that whoever was in the SUV was adequately armed. Something I was not.

I grabbed Allie's hand and pulled her. "Run!" I urged.

When an antelope's flight mode activates, its only response is to sprint away from the danger. The beast's only goal is to escape. The animal is nothing but prey. It has no chance of surviving a full-on confrontation with a lion.

The scenario would be different if it were two lions in a battle. A disadvantaged beast might bolt away from its attacker, but the goal isn't merely escape–it's evasion.

I wasn't an antelope. There was no point in worrying about how helpless I was. Because it wasn't true. I can be deadly when it's needed, even unarmed. Despite that knowledge, I also knew the other lion, no doubt, had at least one gun. Deflecting bullets wasn't an option. I needed a level playing field, and it would not be high noon on the streets of Panama City.

We ran down the block. The sound of the engine roared as the driver pushed the SUV faster. A narrow alley separated two buildings. In my head, I attempted to imagine the layout of the streets. The alley should dump us on the main highway, or what was at least the busier street leading to this district. Of course, that depended on the alley going all the way through.

A chain-link fence with a gate blocked the alley, making it impossible for their vehicle to follow us. My hand released Allie's as I charged the gate. The only thing securing the opening was electrical wire wound around the aluminum fence post. My shoulder rammed the chain-link, bouncing me backward while stretching the wire. I hit it again with all my weight. The thin copper wire snapped in the middle, and the two ends stretched apart, giving us a narrow gap to squeeze through.

Tires squealed behind us. The pounding of our feet on the concrete echoed between the walls. Dark clouds covered up the sun, blocking what little light we had filtering between the buildings. An eerie greenish aura masked everything. It was the kind of green light that comes before a summer storm. In an instant, the air shifted, and I recognized it. I've seen the same climactic change happen almost every day somewhere in South Florida–the afternoon thunderstorm. In Florida, the gale lasts 15 to 20 minutes at most. Sheets of rain dump, leaving thick, sticky air afterward and the recognizable scent of hot, wet concrete.

The jangle of the chain-link resounded down the tunnel. Our pursuers were past the gate. Three hundred feet ahead of me, the alley opened. Cars zipped past the tiny gap in a mere microsecond. Two small dumpsters overflowed with trash near the entrance.

I chanced a look back to see two men running after us. As I suspected, both were carrying weapons. Small automatic pistols that I couldn't identify in the one second glance.

If we cleared the end of the alley, we might have enough witnesses driving along the road to prevent the two men from just gunning us down. Although, I wasn't familiar with Panama. In some countries, gunning people down was common enough that most ignored the crime. By getting involved, they might become a victim themselves. Better to be grateful it wasn't them.

An explosion cracked through the air as the oncoming storm announced its presence.

Come on, I mentally begged the cloud.

As if the sky heard my prayers, the first few drops fell. Big blobs of water came first. Each hitting the ground like volleys from an unseen cannon. The dry dust on the ground exploded up in a small cloud as each drop impacted the concrete. The first onslaught only lasted a few seconds as the wall of rain pressed across the street ahead and into the alley.

Two seconds later, rain engulfed us. The sky turned black, and the sheets of water blinded me.

It also blinded the two men behind us.

"Hang on," I warned Allie as I put both hands on her hips and lifted her up, launching her into the metal dumpster.

She screamed as she vanished into the trash. When she emerged, she'd curse me for it, but the metal can would protect her from stray bullets.

I crouched behind the dumpster. The lid hung somewhat askew over my head, and it deflected some of the rain away. It gave me a small area of clear vision. Enough to see the ground.

The first set of feet appeared. Leather work shoes. The first thing in my head was how uncomfortable they must be. Especially in the rain. The feet shuffled slowly. He knew enough to expect trouble.

I lunged from my hiding spot. The rain covered my eyes, and I blindly caught the man's arms. I wanted to catch his wrists, but I was too high. My hands wrapped around his forearm near his elbow. The goal had been to catch his wrists and twist sharply. The move is used for disarming someone holding a weapon with both hands.

However, if you miss and grab near the elbow, there isn't enough mobility in the arm to wrench the weapon away. It was enough to force the hands down so he wasn't able to fire. The movement drew him closer to me, and I rammed my head into the bridge of his nose. I've heard people say that when you head-butt someone the correct way, then it doesn't hurt. They lie. Most of them are more worried about appearing to be a badass, and they never actually use a head-butt. They hurt every time. It's just a matter of avoiding long term injury.

The initial blow rattled my head, but my forehead cracked something in his nose. I followed up with another one, rattling my brain even more. This time, there was more of a crunch as the cartilage in his nose broke. My right knee shot up and caught him squarely in the groin.

He let out a grunt, and my hands now slid down to his wrist to twist the gun away.

The second man was three feet behind him. Through the rain, I saw him raise his gun. I twisted away from the first man, using his body to shield me as his gun spat out three rapid-fire shots. The shooter's aim put the three rounds in the first man's back.

As he fell forward, my left hand carried the automatic around my front and fired under my right arm. The gun had an automatic setting, firing three shots with each pull of the trigger. I fell to my side as the man collapsed onto me, but I fired three more shots.

My shoulder scraped the concrete as I hit the ground. Shoving the body off me, I rolled away from the two men and raised the gun in my hand. Rainwater dripped down the bridge of my nose, and I blinked to clear the water from my eyes. Two figures were lying on the ground. My hand quivered as I held the gun inches above the ground.

Neither man moved. I waited a full second before letting the barrel of the gun droop. My hands pushed me up.

The rain continued to pour, and I let it wash the grime of the alley off me.

"Are they dead?" Allie asked as her head raised over the lip of the dumpster.

I wasn't sure, but I guessed they were. Warily, I kept the weapon ready as I offered her a hand.

When she was back on the ground, I motioned for her to follow me back the way we came.

"Why?" she asked.

"Their car," I pointed out.

18

18

The subway train rattled as it ripped through the tunnels beneath Panama City.

"Did you know this is the only subway in South America?" Allie rambled almost nonsensically.

"I had no idea," I responded, resting my head against the train's window.

It might have been the only subway, but the train wasn't crowded at the moment. By the time we made it to the station, the rain had stopped. We were still dripping wet, and it appeared we weren't the only ones escaping the weather. The other three riders sat over growing puddles.

"What are we going to do?" Allie mumbled under her breath.

Every fiber of Allie had twisted in a knot. She'd been that way since we left the alley and the two dead men. I wanted to go through their pockets, but it didn't seem prudent. I opted to take their car, but the idea had no legs. We found the SUV locked, and since going back to rifle the dead men's pockets for the keys would take too long, we hoofed it to the main street where we found the subway station.

"Right now, just relax," I urged her.

"Relax!" she snapped. "You just killed two people."

I nodded slowly, making eye contact. "But we are safe."

"I'm wet," she blurted out.

The corner of my mouth lifted, and she smiled, repeating, "I'm wet."

"We need to find some dry clothes, I suppose."

Allie rolled her head onto my shoulder. "I'm sorry," she muttered.

"For what?"

Her right hand reached across her body to squeeze my arm. "I've dragged you into all this. You didn't ask for any of this. I'm betting if you had it to do again, you'd sail away from that plane."

"That doesn't sound like me," I advised. "None of this is your fault. The two men today had every intention of killing us. Don't lose any sleep for them."

I said those words, knowing full well I didn't mean them. But for her, it wasn't a burden she needed to haul around.

"Still," she whispered.

"How about some food?" I suggested. "After you buy me some dry clothes."

She smiled again. "There are some fancy places," she offered. "Panama City has some of the finest restaurants south of the states. We need to get off at the next stop though."

"Where are you taking me?"

"*Casco Viejo*. Means 'Old Quarter.' It's a trendy little area near the water. Lots of restaurants and shops."

"Can we find some dry clothes?" I asked.

She nodded. Her mood had lifted at the thought of hitting the town. It was a technique I bet she'd used before. Mask the problem with lavish living. There are worse ways to hide from one's troubles.

The subway slowed. The inertia swaying our heads forward.

"Come on," she urged. "This is our stop."

When we emerged from the underground, the city was drying off. The sidewalks had a few puddles remaining, but the equatorial sun was evaporating the water almost as fast as it fell.

We hiked two blocks east. I'd say it was reminiscent of the French Quarter in New Orleans, but it had a different ambiance. The architecture was Spanish, with red-tiled roofs on nearly every building. Balconies hung over the bricked sidewalks, many with strings of Edison lights crossing the streets.

The narrow streets were busy as Panamanians were getting off work and filing through the maze of brightly colored buildings. The roads were paved with red bricks, most already dry from the recent downpour. A few pedestrians offered scornful glances my way.

"I forgot I was under-dressed," I remarked.

"First stop," Allie informed me, pointing down the street at an orange building with a window filled with three dapper mannequins.

The air inside the store smelled of lavender and what might have been clover. The interior was small compared to even boutique shops I'd seen in South Florida. Its footprint was less than 1,000 square feet, but by spacing the racks of clothes around in some strategic pattern I would have never comprehended, the shopkeeper created the illusion of an uncrowded space.

Allie led me to a rack of linen pants. She ran her finger along the rack until she found the one she deemed would fit me.

"These are European sizes," she advised me, as if no choice I planned to make would be correct.

I nodded as she handed me a pair of pants. The pale color wouldn't last long, given my general lifestyle. I go through t-shirts like some people use paper towels. Between boat work or the sun and sea, my clothes never fared a long life. Of course, I wasn't a clothes guy. I spent too many years wearing fatigues to care what I looked like on a regular day.

"Here," Allie called, passing me a slick red shirt.

"Is this silk?" I asked, trying to figure out how long it would take me to snag the material.

"You'll look good," she assured me.

I thought about arguing. The price tag had enough zeroes to make me consider trading it for another solar panel.

"You'll fit in," she explained, as if she knew the comments I was thinking. Her eyes locked on mine with determination, and I took the shirt from her.

"Go try them on," she encouraged me, pointing to a room behind the sales counter where a 50-something man watched. He wore a silk shirt and a glare of pure disdain for me. I didn't think he'd side with me in this battle.

Despite my concerns for the cost of the clothes, the thought of dry, clean clothing appealed to me. When I finished buttoning the shirt, I studied myself in the mirror.

"Here," Allie announced as she opened the door.

In her hand was a jacket that she swore complemented the color of my linen pants. I slipped into it before admiring myself in the mirror. It was still not my style, but it felt comfortable. And, honestly, I no longer looked like a panhandler.

"Shoes," Allie blurted out, passing a pair of loafers through the door, followed immediately by a matching leather belt.

By the time I slipped into the shoes and laced the belt through the loops, I stepped out of the room to see Allie wearing a new dress that slid over every curve of her body as if the designer perfectly crafted it for her figure. It took me a good two seconds to notice it was green. In her right hand she held a bag, where I guessed a few other articles of clothing remained hidden.

"Wow," I mumbled.

"You should see me sometime when I have make-up on," she remarked with a smile. "Come on. I've already paid."

She took my wet clothes, balled them up, and put them into a plastic bag. My sandals she stuck in her other bag of clothes, but only after shaking them free of dirt and mud.

She offered the bag to the shopkeeper and asked him something in Spanish. He took the clothes with a smile and a nod.

While I could use a shower, I felt like a new man as we walked out onto the sidewalk.

"Watch your step," she warned as we crossed a small section of sidewalk paved with the kind of ceramic tiles one uses in a shower. I stepped warily across it without slipping.

"That's a design flaw," I commented.

"You'll see it everywhere," she told me. "It's like someone repaired a 500-year-old building with something from the discount aisle at Home Depot."

The afternoon was slowly waning the way any tropical afternoon does. We were on the east coast of Central America, so there were no sunsets over the water here. Still, the red and orange tones burned away the blue sky. In 45 minutes, the air would cool as the stars came out.

"If we hurry," Allie told me, "we can catch the sunset at *Casa Casco*. They have an amazing rooftop bar."

Each stride she made was long and fast, as if she was determined to make it to her destination as quick as she could without breaking into a run. Despite my legs having a few extra inches on hers, I marched at near double-time to keep up with her.

"You'd make a hell of a drill sergeant," I quipped.

"Oh, too much structure for me," she remarked. "Besides, the uniforms are drab."

With that last statement, she took a step forward, twirled like the narrow alley was a catwalk, and offered a glamorous smile.

I snickered, saying, "I think you'd pull off fatigues."

She halted mid-step and kissed me. "I'd pull off yours," she growled as she released my lips.

As swiftly as she kissed me, she was back in step toward a three-story white building. Balconies skirted the top two floors. White concrete railings allowed guests to lean over the streets. A double door sat in the middle of the building. Sculpted in black iron above the doors were the words "*Casa Casco*" with a large "C" over the name.

Allie led me inside to a dining room with checkered floors and a large marbled bar along one side. Shelves of high-end liquors ran along behind the bartender who was talking to a couple with two pink concoctions in martini glasses. The bottles ranged from high-end vodkas to high-end tequilas with a few top-notch rums and, of course, a small selection of Scotch and bourbon.

I started for the bar, when Allie caught me by the sleeve of my brand-new linen jacket.

"We're going to the rooftop," she told me. "Remember. Sunset."

The three flights of stairs took us past three separate dining areas. Each one felt like it had a different theme, but the overarching architecture and decor was decidedly Central American. When we reached the rooftop, I had to admit the view was spectacular. The top of the building was open, with concrete tiled floors and tables scattered around the area. We walked around the roof until we faced the western sky. The ball of red dipped its bottom below the horizon.

"*¿Puedo traerte algo de beber?*" a woman asked in Spanish. I understood "*beber.*" Drink. I guessed she was asking if we wanted something to drink.

My brain wracked through my high school Spanish. I don't think they taught us how to translate "rum."

Finally, I gave up. "Rum, *por favor*. On the rocks. How do you say 'ice?'"

"*Dos Abuelos con hielo,*" Allie translated.

The server nodded with a smile. "Yes," she responded in English.

I laughed as she walked away. "What did you order?"

"Two rums on the rocks," Allie explained. "'*Hielo*' is 'ice.'"

"I thought "*abuelo*" is grandfather?"

Allie grinned. "It is, but it's also the name of a nice local rum."

When the waitress returned, Allie ordered some food. We had a few seconds to toast the sunset before the bright red vanished completely.

The air was cooling now that the sun vanished, and the clouds speckled across the sky broke apart revealing stars glittering down from above us. Allie leaned into my chest. Not quite pressing against me, but the gap between us was nonexistent. My arm wrapped around her shoulder, pulling her even closer. She made a soft murmur as she nestled against me.

While the stars began to twinkle, the lights of Panama City washed out the light show I usually enjoyed when I'm out cruising. Still, the purple sky was beautiful. The few bright twinkles winked down at us.

The server returned with a tray of bacon-wrapped scallops, something Allie must have ordered.

"These don't look Panamanian," I commented.

"Panama has both bacon and scallops," she remarked as she picked one off the tray and popped it into my mouth.

My head turned as I chewed the scallop. The two men who just came up the stairs caught my attention. They were together but wanted to look as if they came separately. Neither were locals. The suits were off-the-rack varietals mass produced overseas and sold in generic department stores. Not that I was one to offer fashion advice.

I turned back and grabbed two more scallops from the tray.

"You'll choke if you eat too fast," Allie joked.

With a smile, I leaned in and kissed her neck, whispering, "Let's walk toward the north side."

I didn't want to point out the two men yet. Instead, I wanted to maneuver us toward the north edge of the roof where a bold red sign marked a fire exit.

Allie nodded and picked up the tray of scallops in one hand while sipping from the tumbler of rum in her other. The two men had identified us as their quarry, but they weren't closing in yet. They appeared to be working their respective ways around either side of us. I offered a fake laugh and kissed Allie's cheek playfully.

"You're suddenly quite flirty," Allie noted. "Was it the rum or the scallops?"

"I'm sure it's just the company," I told her. "The city looks beautiful from up here."

I scanned the streets below. We were on one of the higher buildings in the quarter, but even at that, we only topped the others by a story or two. I couldn't see anyone waiting below on the street. If there were only two of them, it would be easy enough to make a run. If they had back-up, we might run into the hands of the enemy.

I tried to memorize the pattern of breaks in the building that were the alleys and streets. Without a map, I wanted to know which direction to run. We came from the west, and the subway station was somewhere in that direction. That line must have been running mostly north and south, otherwise it would have come closer to the quarter. Although, the city might have intentionally avoided this area for fear of disrupting the historic structures while tunneling.

"Allie," I whispered. "We have two men about to converge on us. I want you to turn around, kiss me, and when you let go, run for the exit door there."

I heard her swallow. But she did what I told her. She spun slowly on one foot, pulled me close, and kissed me. If I hadn't known I gave her instructions, the kiss would have swept me away in that moment. Her lips were soft and electrifying. The moment she broke contact, I was blinking at her back as she bolted through the door.

My senses snapped to me, and I followed her through the door.

19

We were rounding the last flight of stairs when the door on the roof slammed open. At least one of the two men was in pursuit, but we had a solid lead. Allie pushed through the door into the alley.

The alleys of the *Casco Viejo* were poorly lit. The major streets had more lighting, but the shadows overtook the narrow cuts. It was something we could use, and I pushed Allie down the cobbled street.

The map I created in my mind after studying the quarter from above told me to take the next right. It was still a small alley feeding between the old stone buildings. A horn honked as we ran from between the buildings into the street. My hand slammed down on the hood of an old Ford Fiesta as I pushed Allie out of the way. The driver glared at me and pressed on his horn.

I offered him an apologetic wave before running across the street.

"Is that them?" Allie shouted as she glanced back across the street.

My head turned to see the two men from the rooftop coming out of the alley. "Yeah," I responded. "Keep going," I urged.

On my command, Allie ran through an outdoor café and through a wrought-iron gate leading to the next alley. She sprinted ahead, and I turned on our pursuers. There were enough witnesses sitting in the café to discourage them from shooting me there, but it didn't stop me from starting a fight.

As I spun on my foot, the closest man flashed a look of pure shock as I charged him. He'd closed the gap between us, and I only had to bolt about ten feet toward him. My shoulder dropped, turning me into a battering ram. I struck him just below his sternum. The blow sent a concussive wave under his ribs, knocking the wind out of him. The force lifted him off the ground a few inches, and I straightened up after hitting him. He fell backward toward the sidewalk as his companion raced up behind him.

The biggest challenge in hand-to-hand combat isn't the force or strength with which you strike the opponent. That matters, of course. But the deciding factor is often one's stance. The first man was mid-stride when I hit him.

He had no chance to stop the inertia I was driving into him.

As the second man came for me, I skidded to a stop and planted my feet in a perpendicular stance with my right foot forward and my toes aimed ahead of me. My left came down at a right angle, aiming toward the left. The man attempted to tackle me, leaping over his fallen comrade. I caught him as he soared through the air. My torso twisted, throwing him off me.

The customers at the café were on their feet. Several cell phones aimed our direction, taking video of the incident. I'd be featured on numerous social media profiles in just a few minutes.

The second man rolled across the sidewalk and raised to his feet. His hand went under his jacket. A H&K VP9 came out in his grip. The little 9 mm handgun trained on me, and muffled cries sounded from the café behind me as the patrons began scattering.

"Don't move!" the man shouted. "That's enough!"

I lifted my hands up in surrender.

"Dammit Richie," the first man cursed as he pulled himself up off the sidewalk.

"I needed to stop him," Richie offered in defense.

The first man reached into his coat and pulled out a card. I took it from him and read the front, "Saul Almanza.

Agent. Bureau of International Narcotics and Law Enforcement."

"Put it up, Richie," he ordered the second man. Almanza turned to the remaining café patrons and said something in Spanish. He repeated it in English. "This is a police matter. Please return to your meal."

"What the hell is this?" I asked, waving the card.

"Exactly what it says," Almanza told me. "I'm Saul Almanza with the INL. This is Richie Carreón."

I shook my head as I stared at the two men. "INL?"

Almanza pointed at the card. "The Bureau of International Narcotics and Law Enforcement."

Despite the sound of their names, neither man looked like they were Panamanian nor did they speak with an accent. "Do you work for the government of Panama?" I asked.

Almanza shook his head. "No, we are American. We do work with the National Police."

The situation knocked me off my guard. I'd never heard of the Bureau of International Narcotics and Law Enforcement.

"Do you mind if we find Ms. Tremblay and get off the streets?" Almanza asked. "We've caused quite a ruckus."

Glancing around at the café, many patrons had run off, leaving plates of food untouched. The fact the police hadn't shown up yet surprised me. But I was still struggling with a decision to trust this man or not. The vast number of different American agencies operating around the globe would astonish most people. If I never dealt with them, there would be little reason for me to recognize the name.

"Fine," I relented, "but if anyone gets an urge to pull their weapon, all bets are off."

"We understand Mr. Gordon. Richie made a mistake."

Richie protested, "He was coming after me."

Almanza rolled his eyes. "Had you been a foot closer to Mr. Gordon, I think the man would have disarmed you and unloaded your little gun into your scrawny ass."

Richie's demeanor deflated more.

"Where did Ms. Tremblay run off to?"

I shrugged and pointed down the alley. Allie likely stopped somewhere when she realized I wasn't with her. Of course, she could have taken my absence as a sign to keep running.

My first thought was correct. Allie was cowering behind a dumpster when I reached her.

"Chase?" she called.

"It's okay," I promised, although I still was uncertain. "These men say they are with the government."

Her head popped up over the dumpster. "Can they help us?" she asked with relief in her voice.

"That's what they always say," I commented with a dose of snark. "Let's see if they really can."

"Ms. Tremblay, my name is Saul Almanza. I'm with the Bureau of International Narcotics and Law Enforcement."

She looked at me questioningly.

"I thought the same thing," I replied to her. "It's a mouthful."

"That's why we call it the INL," Almanza informed us.

"Why don't you tell us what you do?" I suggested.

"The INL falls under the auspices of the Department of State. We work with the Panama National Police to curtail the traffic of narcotics. This is a major smuggling port with ships heading off in all directions."

"Are you a law enforcement agency?" I asked.

"Not exactly," Almanza explained. "Like I said, we work with the National Police, as well as agents from the FBI, DEA, and even Homeland Security. We don't have any jurisdiction here."

I glanced at Richie. "Which is why pulling a gun on the street is not an INL sanctioned action?"

Almanza nodded. "You'll have to forgive Richie. He was with the California Bureau of Investigation before joining us. He's still getting his sea legs."

Richie grunted.

"Why are you following us?" Allie asked.

"Can we take you back to our offices? We really need to debrief you, and truthfully, you knocked the shit out of me back there. I'd like to get some aspirin."

"Listen, Almanza, can you two give us a minute?"

The INL agent nodded again before ushering Richie back down the alley.

"What do we do, Chase?"

My head turned to check on the two agents. They were standing almost 75 feet away. Richie was talking with both his hands and a lot of facial muscles. Their voices were inaudible.

"I've never heard of the INL," I admitted. "They give off the cop vibe, but if I'm honest, I'm wary."

"Do we run?"

I considered it for a second. They found us pretty quick, which meant they had tabs on where we were the whole time. I didn't notice a tail. They must have very good surveillance, in which case running would only get us away from these two.

"I'm going to leave it up to you," I told her. "If we see what they have to say, it might be more than we already know."

"How much do we tell them?" she asked.

"Leave out the numbers your father left us. In fact, we need to hide them."

She smiled at me. "I thought the same thing." Her eyes cut over to where she had them hidden.

"Good girl," I acknowledged. "I'll leave it up to you."

"Let's see what they have to say," she responded.

"I had a commander who offered a warning. She would tell us to "Tread carefully in the grass where you can't see the snakes.'"

Allie nodded in understanding. I flagged Almanza over.

"Are we in agreement?" he asked cautiously.

"Yeah. Let's hear you out, but we make no promises."

Almanza offered both of his palms as if to say, "Of course."

"I'll want to make a call to the states too," I insisted.

"Once we get to my office, you can make yourself at home."

The two men led us back toward the *Casa Casco* to find a late model Lincoln parked in an alley. Everything about the Lincoln was what one expected a US government bureaucrat to drive in a foreign country. The American taxpayer spent good hard-earned money to ship an American-made car to Panama where it could drive around with no discretion or subterfuge.

Richie manned the wheel. He was the new guy. If he was 30, it would shock me. What would make a young cop want to leave the California Bureau of Investigation to work in an agency that few people were aware existed?

Almanza was different. He checked off the boxes for this kind of gig. There was a scent to him. The Agency. He was older. Mid to late 50s. Perhaps running around the desert was too exhausting for him. Or he wanted a change of pace. Most CIA agents were either career or they found themselves burned out of the work, either by choice or not.

Saul Almanza seemed comfortable here. He'd been out of the CIA for more than a few years. He hadn't gone native. The suit still screamed American. I may have adapted to the Panamanian style quicker.

Richie weaved through the traffic in the quarter until we found ourselves back among the modern architecture. He seemed to possess the ability to avoid the slow crawl of traffic that plagued everywhere I'd seen in the city.

"How long have you been stationed here?" I asked Almanza.

"Been in Panama for the last 20 years. Before I joined the INL, I was with the DEA back in the 90s working in the Bogota office."

I nodded, wondering if there was any truth to that. During the Clinton years, the CIA was clustering their efforts on the drug war. At that time, Al Qaeda was little more than a nuisance. Despite having agents embedded in the Middle East, the government still focused on the pointless war on drugs. One day, someone in the White House or Congress is going to pull some brain cells together to realize that the "War on 'whatever'" is an unwinnable effort. It's terribly difficult to fight the intangible, and when we remove one leader, the perpetual moles pop up with a brand new one to whack.

"I've read your record, Mr. Gordon," Almanza commented. "You have had quite a career."

"Well, I had a career," I retorted. "Not sure it was anything exemplary."

"The Medal of Honor and Purple Heart you received would argue that," Almanza countered.

"A Purple Heart only meant I was good at catching a bullet. The other one required me to lose three members of my team. Nothing about that day was exemplary."

Almanza pursed his lips. There was an unspoken acknowledgment there. His eyes held something else—a new understanding. I revealed something about my character to him, and he realized it. In turn, it revealed Almanza's intuition.

Somehow, I felt more wary.

20

The office Almanza and Richie occupied sat on the third floor of a cheap office building nestled on a busy street filled with banks and insurance offices. Few people walked the concrete paths between the buildings. These sidewalks were sparse, likely a result of the six parking garages on the different corners of the avenue. The worker bees in this neighborhood were commuters, driving upscale sedans and SUVs.

Most of the architecture in this area was from the 70s and early 80s. Buildings poured from large turning vats of concrete stood like dingy cliff walls. Tinted windows lined the cliffs like an exhibit in a herpetarium with lizards crawling up the glass in futile efforts to escape their confines. It was claustrophobic, but with a view of the other captives.

The INL office had missed out on whatever budgetary funds might have transitioned it into the next decade. Wood-paneled walls built the decade I was born still enclosed the office. Short industrial carpet had been walked on until it was threadbare and faded. It felt like a department forgotten by the latest tax increase. I wondered if it was because so few tax-payers ventured into this realm, although I realized even the makeshift trailers and tents used in Afghanistan were better decorated.

As far as I could tell, the only occupants of the office were the two INL agents. There were three desks, but one had the appearance of disuse. Sure, papers, files, and books filled the desktop, but the normal area where one actually worked wasn't clear. Even the most cluttered and disorganized person needs to move their piles to write or type. It's unconscionable to attempt to type on a keyboard that is thrown off-kilter by useless files.

There were three rooms, but two of the doors remained closed. Deadbolt locks on the outside indicated the rooms may be used for holding people, either for questioning or in custody. The third room simply led to a small kitchen where a coffee-pot, microwave, and refrigerator waited for use.

"Richie, why don't you put them in the interrogation room?" Almanza suggested.

Richie paused for a split second, as if trying to comprehend what the older agent told him. Then he pointed us toward one of the rooms with the locks on the door. "Follow me," he ordered.

I paused, eying the door.

Almanza commented, "It's just what we call it. There are just more chairs. We can sit down and talk."

Allie glanced at me, and I just shrugged. At this point, I wasn't sure what push back we might get. My guess is there wasn't a lot of authority in this office. That didn't mean a quick phone call to the Panama National Police wouldn't land us in a less comfy jail cell.

She moved toward the door as Richie opened it. Inside was a large wooden table with six chairs around it. In another world, it could have been a conference table for a small company. Here it felt too large for the room.

"Almanza," I called. "I'm still going to want to make a phone call."

"Oh, of course," he responded. "Follow me."

I gave Allie a nod before following Almanza to the second closed door. He unlocked it and turned on the lights. It was the same size as the interrogation room, but instead of a large table, it held a single desk with a phone and computer. Unlike the other desk in the communal area, this one had nothing besides the phone and computer. I stepped into the office and ran my fingers over the computer. The back of the monitor had a collection of dust forming on the back.

"Just dial out," Almanza told me.

I picked up the receiver, and the agent milled around the communal area. After a second, I stepped to the door and pulled it closed, offering me a better degree of privacy.

The number I dialed was filed in my memory. One of three numbers for Judith Shaw I knew by heart. My former commander would not be that easy to track down. Since she took a job at the Pentagon a few years ago, I'd spoken to her twice. Both times required going through another party to get the message to her.

Still, I'd be remiss not to at least try.

The first number rang six times before I hung up. Shaw still had a landline at her house, but the chances of getting her there were virtually nil. I tried the second number. A corporal picked up. I missed his name, but all I really needed was his rank. She wasn't in the office, and short of being the president or a five-star general, he wasn't about to give me a time frame she could get back to me. I'd be lucky if the message made it to her this week.

The third number was likely my best shot. I dialed the Iowa area code.

"Hello?" a woman answered.

"Hi, Emily. This is Chase Gordon," I told her.

"Oh," the woman responded, as she recognized my name. "The Lieutenant."

"Yes, ma'am."

"You want my mother?" Emily Shaw asked.

"Yes."

"She's in Germany." It was a statement not an excuse. Shaw was unavailable. At least for the moment.

"I'm tangled up in something in Panama," I told Emily. "I wanted to ask the General about the INL."

"The what?" the school teacher asked.

I tried to line up the words in my head as I explained, "The Bureau of International Narcotics and Law Enforcement."

"Does she work with them?" the woman asked.

"I doubt it. I'm just curious what she knows."

"How can she reach you?" Emily asked. A question with no actual answer.

"Going to be hard. I'll call you back later. When do you think you'll hear from her?"

"I don't know, Lieutenant Gordon."

"It's just Chase, these days."

Emily cleared her throat. "Chase," she tested the name. "I'm not sure how or why you endeared yourself to my mother. She's had a lot of men under her command."

"It's difficult to explain," I told her.

"I don't really care," she responded. "My mother is the most powerful woman I know. Just make sure you don't put a chink in her armor."

"No, ma'am," I promised.

"Good," she replied. I appreciated the protective shield she wanted to put around Shaw. For a kindergarten teacher, a mother like General Shaw must seem almost omnipotent. How do you protect someone all-powerful?

"Chase, maybe one day you'll come visit," she suggested. It wasn't a request. Nor did it sound like a demand. More like an inquiry to a long-lost sibling. She wanted to understand Shaw's relationship with me. Was I like a brother or an uncle? Perhaps Shaw and I were lovers—a chance for the career General to find some personal balance. That might be enough to keep her close to home and her daughter. None of that was close to accurate.

When I heard the click, I forgot I was on the phone.

"Shit!" I cursed.

"What is it?" Emily asked.

"I'm a damned idiot!" I exclaimed. "Sorry, Emily, I have to go."

"Chase, what's goin—" The line went dead before I hung up.

I cursed my stupidity. Almanza played me. Had he shut the door, I'd have been immediately suspicious.

In a single stride, I crossed the room and turned the door knob. The deadbolt secured me inside the office.

"Damn! Damn! Damn!" I shouted. "Allie!"

I couldn't hear anything in the other room. My arrogance let me drop my guard. I convinced myself I was smarter than Almanza. Instead, I'm locked in an office while they do whatever with Allie.

My shoulder rammed into the door. Fruitless. The door swung inward, and the door jamb and deadbolt were suppressing any blow I dealt it. Even the hinges were encased in the frame. I couldn't get to them without chopping away half the door.

I grabbed the phone again, hoping the line was no longer dead.

No luck.

The computer.

Damned thing wasn't even plugged to the wall.

My foot slammed against the door. Over and over. With no effect.

I should have dropped them both on the street. No, you dumbass. You let them play you. Probably right down to Richie, pulling his gun. He had the drop on me.

Almanza said it. If he tried to take me by force, I'd stand a good chance of disarming Richie and turning the tables. I should have sensed it. I guess I did. There wasn't a moment of trust with them, but I still let Almanza separate us. He let me spend an hour with him in the car. Get comfortable with my distrust.

I'll kill him.

Where would they take Allie? They didn't want her alive. Which means they don't want me alive.

Why not just kill me here?

They don't want us dead yet. It's the only thing that makes sense. Contain me while they secure Allie somewhere else. If they have her, they think I'll be easier to control.

Time to get out, Gordon.

The door would not budge. How long would they need to get Allie away and come back? Half an hour. Unless one of them is still here, waiting for me.

Would they wait to open up the door with just one of them? I didn't think so. Not unless they could ensure my cooperation.

My right hand wrenched the phone off the desk and hurled it against the paneled wall opposite the door. The plastic telephone shattered against the wood paneling, leaving only a slight scratch in the veneer.

They controlled the telephone from outside of the office. It only made sense they'd want to use it to communicate with me before they came inside. Subdue me with threats against Allie before they ever unlocked the door.

If that was their plan, I just rewrote it. No phone. No subduing.

Some might suggest keeping communication going was the best way to find Allie. I don't agree. At some point, Allie's life is forfeit, no matter what. The question was, would mine be as well.

If I did as they asked, I might find an opportunity to attack. That's a lot like losing at chess. Once the game turns, a player finds himself on the defensive. A single king running around the board might end the game in a draw, but the king will never get checkmate.

One thing the Corps implanted in my head was a draw was never good enough.

I'd removed the line of communication. The big unknown was if someone was waiting outside the door.

If they were, it changed little. If they left me alone, thinking I was secure enough. Well...that gave me a window. Time to go after their pawns.

The door would not open without some help from the outside or, at the very least, an enormous crowbar.

My eyes turned up to the ceiling. Nicotine-stained acoustic tiles hung from metal grids. A smile crept across my face.

My first instinct was to tear through the wood paneling. That veneer was at least thirty years old. Even in the protected confines of the office building, the tropical weather would leave the wood brittle and easy to break.

However, the ceiling offered another opportunity.

I suspected this "office" was mostly a prop. If Almanza and Richie were INL, it was a futile post. This probably wasn't the actual INL office. It was a lure to trap stupid boat bums with their heads up their asses.

The point, though, is that above the ceiling is often unfinished. Drywall might cover walls above the grid, but no one in their right mind is putting wood paneling up there.

When I climbed on the desk, I took a little too much pleasure in kicking the computer to the floor. The crack of the monitor gave me a sick sense of pleasure.

Ceiling grid like this is nothing more than metal pieced together in a square. The entire structure is held up by the edge and a few strands of wire that tie it to steel crossbeams or concrete anchors. Which means when a pissed off boat bum pulls his head out of his ass, he can grab pretty much anywhere and pull down.

With a loud crash, half the ceiling came down onto the floor of the office. Ceiling tiles fell to the floor. Flat metal rods clattered off the desk and floor. Two pieces remained in each of my hands. They were about two feet long, with a tapered end that formed a sharp point.

With the ceiling effectually gone, I heard movement in the other office. In my mind, I imagined Richie standing with his gun pointed at the door, waiting on it to give way.

My eyes swept above me. Steel girders ran along the concrete, securing the floor above me. The railing was about a foot too high for me to reach from where I stood.

The two metal spears I held would make ideal weapons, and I had no intention of ditching them. Instead, I slid each through a belt loop on either side of my waist before I dropped to the floor, looking like some cheap version of a samurai.

I lifted the edge of the desk and took a run toward the door. A screech howled as the legs of the desk slid across the floor. It ended abruptly as the desk slammed into the door with a resounding crash.

From the other side of the door, the pop of a gunfire was muffled at first, but the second shot was louder. The wooden door absorbed the futile shots.

Richie must be anxious.

With a heave, I upended the desk against the door. The following thud didn't bring anymore gunshots.

I scaled the desk until I reached the summit. With the desk on end, I could reach the girder with little effort.

What was poor Richie thinking?

Once I grabbed the steel railing, I climbed to the opposite wall, where I could rest my feet on the top of the wood paneling. The wall stretched all the way to the outer hallway, where a tall drywall barrier prevented me from reaching the hall.

My feet shuffled along the ledge as my hands moved from girder to support bars. When I reached a position over the next room, I bent my knees while maintaining my balance. I lifted the ceiling tile closest to me. The room below was empty except for a wooden table with five chairs around it.

The table was in the center of the room—too far to jump to. I'd have to drop all the way to the floor. There would not be a quiet way to do that, and Richie was already on edge. Any way I did it, I'd be crashing through the metal grid and ceiling tiles.

Both hands drew the metal spears from the last ceiling from my belt. Armed, I took a leap. More of a drop. With some precision, I let my feet land on two intersections of grid, allowing my weight to rip it apart and leave the largest hole.

Metal clanged to the ground as I landed on the tiled floor. I charged toward the door but slid to a stop on my knees just to the right of the opening.

As if on cue, gunfire erupted in the hallway. Splinters of wood sprayed from the door as 9 mm slugs shredded holes in the door. Four rapid-fire shots penetrated the door at what would have been chest height. The knob made an ever-so-slight squeak as it turned.

Richie pushed the door open about two inches–enough to grab the edge with my left hand and jerk it open. The makeshift spear in my right hand drove up and rose through the door. Richie was still pushing the door open when the sharp edge burrowed under his ribs. The 9 mm exploded in his hand. A last desperate measure.

I didn't feel the impact of the bullet at first. Not really.

Instead, I flew backward in a slow-moving fall. Before I hit the ground, the blow to my chest burned.

I stared at the broken ceiling, wondering if the lights would fall now that the grid lost its structural integrity. My eyes blinked, and my chest burned.

21

There wasn't any air in the room. At least none I could get into my lungs. My chest heaved slowly, trying to inhale anything.

There's a feeling when one's held their breath past the point they are comfortable, when the lungs burn out a cry for more air. This was worse. It was as if I could taste the air. My body knew it was there, but it seemed to be useless. I continued to gasp.

My fingers reached for my chest. Warm, sticky blood clung to the fingertips. I held my hand up. The dark blood covered the palm.

Shit.

The bullet hole was right over my left lung.

No air. Punctured lung.

Shit. Shit.

How long can I live without a lung?

You still have one lung, a voice in my head reminded. That means you should be able to breathe.

I wasn't sure how lungs worked in that fashion. I remember a neighbor when I was younger who lost a lung to cancer. She survived on one lung.

Get up, Chase.

I ignored the voice. Instead, I stared at the broken ceiling above me.

Of course, my neighbor had it removed, not blown apart by a hollow-point slug. There would be different consequences to that kind of thing.

Shit, I could be drowning in my own blood. How did that feel? Could the blood get from one lung to the other?

Get the fuck up, Gordon.

That voice sounded like Shaw. Instinctively, I rolled to my right. Each breath was laborious and painful.

Maybe I should just wait for help.

Who's coming back? Almanza? He won't help you.

My right arm pushed me up. Each movement was like a kick to the chest. Was the bullet still in me? Did it exit?

No time to think. I crawled toward Richie's body. The metal piece of grid extruded from his chest. I'd done more than puncture his lung. The thrust should have ripped his liver open, at the very least.

His hand still gripped the 9 mm. My right arm dragged me closer. The entire left side of my torso hurt.

It wasn't the first bullet I'd taken. That didn't ease the pain. The knowledge didn't help me at all. If I didn't get help, I'd still die. Slowly and painfully, but dead is dead.

Plus, there was Allie.

Almanza took her somewhere. I planned to kill him when I found him.

Not if you don't get up, Gordon.

I pulled the 9 mm from Richie's hand. He still had six rounds in the magazine.

Where was the cavalry when you needed it?

Something nagged at me from the back of my brain. Between the voice of Shaw telling me to get moving and the image of Allie in danger, I had trouble focusing.

Someone would be back. Probably Almanza. I needed to get him to take me to Allie before it was too late.

I laid the gun on the floor and used the door jamb to pull myself up into a seated position. My back rested against the wall where I crouched earlier. My head lolled back against the nicotine-stained wall-paper.

The police. I should call the police. Except the phone was in the next room.

You broke it, you idiot.

My head twisted to stare at Richie. He'd have a phone. Didn't I see him use it earlier? It was a faint memory. It might have been nothing but my imagination, but it was a safe bet. Everyone had a phone. Except me. I'd die here in this shitty, grimy office for lack of a cell phone.

Richie was on my left. That side of me wasn't very useful.

My left arm moved toward the man. The muscles in my chest screamed as every movement pulled at the wound. I gasped for air, feeling like it was to no avail. When my fingers finally gripped Richie's jacket, I didn't have the strength to pull him closer. I let out a howl of defeat.

When the 10-year-old Taliban kid shot me in the back, the bullet tore through muscle and broke my shoulder. It wasn't quite like this. Now, it wasn't just the bullet, but the punctured lung left me flailing like a snapper in the cockpit.

Viener.

If I could get Viener, he might save Allie.

You still need a phone, Chase.

Dammit.

Either I moved or I died. But if I moved, my heart would pump more blood. It felt like a no-win scenario.

A stray thought occurred to me. If I died, no one would pay the dockage fee for *Carina*. Someone would end up buying her for pennies. No one I knew had any idea that she was in Montego Bay.

If I died here, maybe the Panamanian police would notify my family. That would piss my mother off.

Who would tell Jay or Missy?

Here's an idea, Gordon. Don't fucking die.

Every muscle in my body tightened as I threw myself toward the left, landing on Richie's corpse. Tears welled in my eyes as I fought against the pain. The fingers on my right hand crawled over his body, searching for a phone.

In his right pants pocket, I found an iPhone. I didn't have the strength to roll back over. Instead, I remained draped across the dead man.

The phone was locked. The biometric scan needed his face. I shoved the phone up toward Richie's face.

A little check-mark appeared in a circle that started glowing as it loaded.

"Face ID failed," the message told me.

I tried again, straightening his head so the phone had a full view of his features.

The check-mark started glowing again. This time, the entire symbol changed colors, and the word "Success" flashed across the screen.

Viener's number was in my left pocket. There wasn't much chance my right hand would contort that way, either. Certainly not in this position.

I took a deep breath, feeling like metal was scraping the inside of my chest. My right elbow pushed me up off Richie, and I moved my left hand toward my pocket.

A pained grunt emitted from my throat with every movement I made. The number came out of my pocket between my index and middle fingers.

Stretched across the dead man as if we were in some intimate embrace, I dialed the number. The phone rang six times before I hung up.

With no hope, I resigned myself to call the Panamanian police. For a second, I wondered if 9-1-1 worked or was it something different like the UK where it was 9-9-9. The phone rang, interrupting the stray thought.

"Hello," I answered.

"You called?" a voice asked.

"Viener?"

"Gordon?" he responded. "Is that you?"

"I've been shot!" I blurted out.

"Shit!" the old Marine whistled through the phone. "Where are you?"

Before I gave him the location, the outside door opened.

The phone fell from my hand, and I reached back to grab the 9 mm.

"Gordon?" I heard Viener shout through the phone as I raised the gun.

Almanza came through the door. He must have glimpsed Richie spread out on the floor. The door slammed shut before I lined the sights on him.

"Gordon, are you there?" Viener's voice continued to come from the speaker.

I couldn't answer. Even if Almanza saw Richie, it didn't mean he saw me or my condition. If he thought he had the upper hand, he might charge in to finish the job Richie failed.

My breathing was growing harder and harder. My heart rate jumped up as the adrenaline which normally prepared me to fight now caused my body to beg for more oxygen.

My eyes closed slowly.

Most stand-offs are a waiting game. Who has the least patience? Under ideal circumstances, the answer is almost always "me." Right now, it didn't matter. I couldn't go far, and it was only a matter of time before Almanza stepped back through the door to investigate.

Unfortunately, I couldn't go anywhere. If he waited long enough, I was going to pass out, either from blood loss or lack of oxygen. At that point, it wouldn't matter who out waited the other. He'd win. I'd be dead. Allie would be dead.

The room was spinning, as if I'd been on my eighth or ninth tequila shot. My eyes tightened, focusing on the handle of the office door. Everything in my peripheral vision rode a slow wave up and down, but I tried to keep the handle steady. The barrel of the 9 mm drooped as I tried to hold it up.

My brain started counting. I wasn't sure how long after Almanza slammed the door, but several seconds passed before the timer started.

Ten seconds.

Another five.

I blinked slower. My grip loosened on the gun. As soon as I realized it, I tightened my hold, like trying to stay awake on the interstate at night. I knew I couldn't do it much longer.

45 seconds passed.

My fingers slacked, letting the 9 mm hang loose.

Wake up, Gordon.

The handle moved. Or was it everything else moved.

No, it was turning.

The door flew open followed by three gunshots. I blinked again. The 9 mm in my hand was hot. I didn't know if I fired or not. Almanza was holding his chest as he slid against the facing on the door. He slipped to the floor, staring at me with vacant eyes.

"Gordon!" a voice called to me.

I looked for the source. The 9 mm slumped forward, and I closed my eyes.

You have to save Allie, a voice told me.

"I don't know where she is," I responded. My words were muffled as my face pressed into Richie's abdomen.

"Gordon! Can you hear me?"

Viener. He was on the phone.

Gordon, give him your coordinates.

"I don't know them," I mumbled into Richie's blood soaked shirt.

The copper taste of blood was filling my mouth. Was it my blood or Richie's?

"Viener!" I tried to shout.

For a moment, I thought about *Carina*. Maybe I'm on board with Missy.

I didn't hear the ocean. Just the low hum of the florescent lights and my own wheezing breath in my ears.

"Gordon!"

I closed my eyes, thinking about the sun on my skin.

22

The florescent lighting overhead had changed. My eyes opened a little more. It took an effort, but I pushed through the fog.

A fog filled my scrambled brain. I was on a beach.

Or not. My head tried to pull out of the dream.

My arm itched, but I couldn't move to scratch it.

The glow blinded me. My eyes closed again, trying to shield the pale, deathly light shining down.

After I opened them again, the lights had gone out. The room wasn't dark. An orange glow flashed through the room.

My head turned a little. I lay in a bed. A hospital bed. There was a constant beeping from somewhere. I still felt an itch.

No, not an itch. An intrusion.

As the lights flashed, I scanned my arm to see the needle protruding from it.

Everything blurred, and yet, it also seemed so clear.

Richie shot me. I remember trying to get to his gun.

"Look who's awake," a woman's voice broke through the darkness.

A silhouette filled an opened doorway to my left. Her obvious feminine shape moved toward me, but in the low light, I couldn't distinguish her features.

"Allie?" I questioned.

"No," she denied. "How are you feeling?"

"What happened?" I tried to say. The words seemed to fall over my lips. At that moment, I realized my tongue seemed to fill my mouth.

"Rest, Mr. Gordon," she demanded. "It's good you're alert, but let's keep the questions until morning."

"Where am I?" I blathered almost incoherently.

The woman appeared to have no trouble understanding me. She'd conversed with more than a few blubbering fools in her time. Instead of responding, she adjusted something behind my shoulder.

For a second, I made out her face in the repetitive flash of orange. My brain tried to hold the image, but darkness swallowed me again.

"Is he awake?" a voice bellowed. Male. I guessed the owner to be middle-aged. 43. If someone wagered me.

"Not yet, Mr. Fretsh."

Fretsh. I rolled the name around in my head, looking for a match. I drew a blank, but given the sludge through which I mentally tried to swim, I would be lucky to remember my mother's name.

Carla. Carla Gordon.

I remembered. If names had a flavor, hers tasted like an under-ripe persimmon. Sour and pithy to the point of inedible.

A realization washed over me. Someone had called her. Probably not her. They would have called my sister. She'd have told my mother, who would be on the first train to soak up the attention. A dying son would put her in the spotlight she thought she deserved.

"Mr. Gordon?" the woman from earlier spoke when she saw my eyes open.

I didn't respond. My eyes moved around the room. Daylight filled the room, allowing me to see it better than when I woke up last night.

It didn't resemble a normal hospital room. In fact, if not for the hospital bed, I'd have taken it for a regular bedroom. A greenish-brown, leaning toward tan, covered the walls. The windows weren't large paned things one finds in tall buildings. These were 10-paned windows that open outward. The kind you find in a home, albeit not a house in the Ozarks. One might find them in parts of Florida. It had a Spanish feel to the design.

Dumbass, you're in Panama.

It made sense I'd still be there. Richie shot me in the chest.

My chest.

I glanced down at my torso. Shirtless, but white gauze covered the left side. The bandages taped to my skin with clear first-aid tape. The bit of hair I did sport there looked to be shaved off. Or ripped off.

"Can you talk, Mr. Gordon?" the woman asked.

She didn't dress like a nurse, but she still wore a utilitarian dress. The man stood behind her. Thick, like he had once been in prime shape, but the years had made him soft. But he was tall. At least six feet. And he kept his hair cut short, but the tight curls started growing back. He didn't like the curly hair, so he kept it neatly trimmed. Right now, he was on the back side of a haircut. I doubted he would wait another day before he trimmed it.

I got close to his age–definitely between 40 and 45. He wore thin glasses that slid toward the tip of this nose. Within a minute, he'd pushed them up on the bridge twice.

"What happened?" I asked. My words came out clearer than they had last night.

The woman stole a look at Mr. Fretsh, who stepped forward.

"You were shot," he reminded me. "Do you remember that?"

I stared at him. He was an unknown, although he made me think CIA. Still, Almanza reminded me of the same thing. That didn't work out for me.

"I get it," he tried to soothe me. "You don't trust me."

My eyes went to his hands. They were well-manicured. He took a lot of pride in his looks. I bet he tried to get rid of the squishy center, but age was making the fight harder.

"Who are you?" I rasped.

"Can you give us the room, Tammy?" he asked the woman.

She nodded in return and walked out, closing the door behind her.

"My name is Alex Fretsh."

"What agency?" I questioned, narrowing my eyes.

He grinned. "How long did it take you to figure that out?"

"You exude it like the aroma of dead fish."

"That's hurtful," he commented.

I nodded my chin. "It's how I intended it."

"CIA."

I didn't respond.

"I've worked with Eric Viener in the past. He called me asking for my help to find you."

"Where is Viener?" I asked.

"He'll be around later. You can verify anything you want with him."

I didn't mention that Viener and I were only barely acquainted. He was a Marine, but he'd grayed the lines he played in. Of course, perhaps we all do. To some extent.

Fretsh studied me. After a second, he explained, "You left the line open. That's likely what saved your life."

I didn't remember calling anyone. Or maybe I did. Everything still seemed mashed together.

"The men you killed were with an agency called the Bureau with International Law and Narcotics Enforcement."

I didn't respond. At least, he confirmed that.

He continued, "It seems they were moonlighting, too. However, we aren't sure with whom?"

It seemed an easy guess. The Soria Cartel. Perhaps, Steven Clark and Banyan Freight.

"I guess you know, though. Right?" Fretsh asked after watching my face.

"I don't," I lied.

He pursed his lips, nodding as if he didn't know I was lying.

"Where am I?" I asked.

"Safe house. We use it for emergencies. You have...Or rather, you had a collapsed lung. I'll let Tammy cover your prognosis with you in a minute. The bullet punctured your lung and broke a few ribs. As I understand it, you were lucky. The exit wound missed your spinal cord. Tammy says you should recover."

"How long have I been here?"

"Two weeks."

"Two weeks?"

"Given our lack of facilities, we kept you in an induced coma."

"But..." I began.

"Allie Tremblay?" Fretsh used Allie's name as if it was a question he knew the answer to.

My eyebrows lifted.

"The police found her body about 30 kilometers south of the city."

The wind rushed out of me as my heart crashed. My eyes closed.

"I'm sorry, Gordon," Fretsh offered.

"Get out," I muttered.

"Okay," he agreed, retreating through the closed door.

I stared at the ceiling. Allie was dead. Was she dead when Almanza returned to the office?

That was two weeks ago. I'd been out for two weeks.

My fingers found the lift controls on the bed, and I pushed the button to raise my torso. The movement pulled against the bandage, but it didn't hurt as much as I thought it might. Of course, it had two weeks to heal up.

Rage was burning inside me. I got her killed. The events were pouring in now. All the mish-mash of things started clearing up.

It was my fault.

Fucking Almanza left the trap door open, and I walked right into it.

I wanted to kill him.

Too late, you already did.

I stared at the closed door. Fretsch wanted something. Otherwise, he could have taken me somewhere other than a safe house. There wasn't a US military base in Panama, but it would have made sense to send me to a regular hospital. Even with the two dead INL agents, the CIA could smooth something over. Or worst-case scenario, they just let the police deal with me.

No, there was something the CIA wanted out of this.

If he was CIA. Now, my distrust had grown to monstrous proportions.

I didn't care what Fretsh wanted. He could have it. Unless it didn't include killing Steven Clark and the Soria Cartel. In that case, he'd be shit-outta-luck.

The door opened, letting Tammy stick her head inside.

"I'm going to check your wound," she informed me.

My head rolled back as Tammy attempted to remove the tape and gauze from my skin without too much pain. I didn't notice. Instead, I watched the pale light, wondering what happened to Allie.

"I heard you were a Marine," Tammy commented, attempting to make small talk with the patient.

"Yeah," I responded blandly.

She pressed her palm against the hole, which had healed significantly while I was unconscious.

"It's looking great," she told me. "I'm going to change the dressing to a smaller bandage. We want to monitor you for any infection, but it's healing exactly how we want it."

"How long do I need to stay here?" I asked.

"You just woke up, Mr. Gordon."

"Call me Chase," I corrected. "I don't care, though. There are some things I need to attend to."

"I want you to stay in bed through tomorrow. After that, we can walk you around. Build your strength up."

Tammy pulled her auburn hair back in a pony-tail. Her eyes glittered blue with flecks of green glinting in the pale artificial light. In the sunlight, those bits would glisten like emeralds.

"Are you my doctor?" I asked.

"And your nurse and orderly, too," she remarked.

"You CIA too?"

"Something like that," she answered as she used a sterile cloth to clean around the wound.

'Something like that' was vague enough to cover a slew of options. She might simply be someone they keep on-call for emergencies. How big is the CIA's operation in Panama now? Thirty years ago, it would have been a lot, but nowadays, I wondered what the point was.

Of course, the Canal might be a choke point for a lot of things coming into the US. I could speculate all day.

"Do I call you Dr. Tammy?" I asked. "Or do you have a last name?"

"Tammy is fine," she informed me. "Dr. Tammy sounds like a pediatric dentist."

"Did you hear about the girl I was with?" I asked.

Tammy's eyes locked with mine. She shook her head. At least a bit of untruth. Her eyes told me she knew enough to be sorry for me.

"What do you think about Fretsh? Have you worked with him before?"

She applied a smaller bandage over the bullet hole and began taping it to my skin.

"You'll end up with a nice little scar there," she told me, ignoring my queries about Fretsh.

"It can join the collection."

Her veneer cracked with a half-smile. "I noticed a few."

"I doubt you saw them all," I stated.

"I never do," she told me.

Padrino's sat on a block in Miami with vacant buildings and failed businesses surrounding it like the soulless faithful. It was a small oasis in an otherwise desolate section of Miami. It had become a destination for those upscale foodies longing for authentic Cuban fare. Fresh linen covered each table, and it was changed between each guest. The staff polished every piece of silverware daily.

The prices, though, didn't reflect the affluence the decor portrayed. Julio Moreno wanted a restaurant for the average denizen of the neighborhood. When it became a popular destination, he insisted the establishment match the aesthetics of other Miami fine dining establishments. If you were an outsider, the menu differed from the one they gave the locals who only walked from a block over for the *Ropa Vieja*.

Padrino's was also the throne room for Moreno. The corner table was occupied only by Moreno and his underlings. Sectioned off from the rest of the dining room by an ornate partition, the round table was the business center of the Moreno Cartel. Julio and his right-hand henchman, Esteban Velasquez, oversaw most of the drug trade in Florida. His ever-expanding empire was creeping both north and west.

I leaned against the bar and watched as the newest hostess, a second-generation high-school senior, walked with trepidation toward the king and his subjects. She knew who owned and operated the restaurant, and he was never to be disturbed. Certainly not by a white guy who asked for him by his first name.

It had been three weeks since I woke up in the make-shift hospital room. Even after getting an all clear from Tammy, I had no strength. The weeks of confinement to a bed left me atrophied.

Fretsh seemed to linger around the house, and on several occasions, he attempted to delve more into Allie's death. It seemed odd, and I wasn't sure what his end goal was. However, I'd dealt with enough of his kind to know when I'm being played. He all but suggested a full-frontal assault of Banyan Freight and the Soria Cartel. My suspicion was the cartel might be running against the interests of the CIA. Whatever his goal was, I didn't trust him. It didn't matter what he wanted, I had my own goals. If he was lucky, they'd align.

As soon as I was able, I wanted to get away from Fretsh. While Tammy was a nice distraction, I couldn't shake the images my brain concocted of Allie in the last few minutes of her life.

When I'd had enough of the temporary hospital and could move around, I left. Under the radar, Viener flew me to Belize, where I holed up in a small hotel for a week. I dedicated that time to rebuilding some core strength. It was slow-going, as the muscles were tender and weak. After a week, I was back to running five miles a day. Not that I did that regularly before the shooting, but I could at least do it.

Despite the care and time I'd received from Tammy, the wound had not completely healed, and I needed to avoid anything that could cause an infection. Meaning no swimming in the ocean, something I considered necessary for my mental well-being. All of my runs and workouts ended on a shoreline. Those hours watching the surf reminded me of the night on Swan Island.

During those weeks, I couldn't rid my thoughts of Allie. We'd only known each other a few days, but there was a lot of blame and guilt bearing down on me. When I thought about how tired I was after a couple of miles, those emotions drove me onward.

The guilt was overcome by the one major emotion burning through me—rage. Steven Clark sat in an office somewhere in Toronto, ruling over a kingdom he stole. Whether the Soria Cartel worked for him or the other way around, it didn't matter to me. They were as guilty as Clark.

When I wasn't conditioning my body and healing, I used the hotel's computer, spending hours crawling around the web, looking for both Clark and the cartel.

Clark was easy. Banyan Freight's main office sat on the corner of a downtown Toronto intersection. His office had been on the 16th floor, but now that old man Tremblay and his heir were deceased, he might move up a floor. A Wall Street Journal article announced the board promoted Steven Clark to CEO after the untimely deaths of Allison Tremblay and her father. His wife, Sarah, was the majority shareholder, but as she was in a vegetative state, Steven Clark would manage her shares.

Clark seemed to get what he wanted. Unfortunately for him, he did not know I was still alive. When Alex Fretsh pulled me from the INL offices, he arranged for the police to report the discovery of three bodies. The story was headline news in Panama for a week. In the US, it garnered a 30-second blip on all the news networks for one day. America didn't care who died in some Central American country, even if it was members of some unknown bureaucratic agency.

The Panamanian police never identified the third victim, leaving me nameless. That was fine by me. The people I wanted to believe I was dead did, and no one was going to deliver reports of my death to my friends and family in the states. As far as they are aware, I'm sitting on *Carina* somewhere. I hadn't even contacted the dock in Jamaica. They'd rack the bill up until I returned. If that didn't happen soon enough, *Carina* would be sold to pay for the past due fees. I didn't want that to happen, but surfacing to take care of that kind of business might pop me up on someone's radar.

I wasn't ready for that to happen just yet.

A few seconds after announcing me, the young hostess straightened as a six-foot tall man rose to his feet. The scar cutting across his face gave him a menacing glare. It was also the feature that caused me to give him the moniker Scar. I didn't call him that, especially after learning his name. Esteban Velasquez wasn't a man to find humor at his expense. I didn't want to go to battle with him over my insensitivity.

Velasquez motioned for me to come over. He stared at me as I crossed the dining room.

"Gordon," he grunted.

"Esteban, my friend," I greeted the enforcer with a smile. "How have you been?"

The man nodded to me as if that was an answer to everything I asked.

"Chase!" Moreno exclaimed. "Come have a seat. It's been awhile since I've seen you. I do hope you are looking for work?"

"Julio." I used Moreno's first name, something that irked Scar. Someone like Moreno thrives on respect. My refusal to call him "Mr. Moreno" was an effort to keep myself on a level playing field with the man. He had attempted to persuade me to do a few odd jobs for him. I didn't like the way he did his business, and those odd jobs might turn into felonies with little effort. I thought it best to ensure Moreno never suspected he was over me.

"I'd like some information," I told him.

"Information?" Moreno questioned. He motioned for me to take a seat. "Esteban, it seems Chase only ever wants information from me."

"*Sí.*"

"The Soria Cartel." I said the name and leaned back as if it was an offer rather than a question.

Moreno glanced past me to Scar. I couldn't see the enforcer's face, but based on Moreno's eyes, I intrigued him.

"The Sorias," Moreno almost whispered, feigning ignorance. "Why would I know anything about them?"

"Julio, come on now. It's been a couple of years since we first met," I told the man. "There is a DEA van sitting a block down the street just praying that somehow you're going to get a shipment of cocaine in with the pork. It's the same van that was sitting there a year ago when I came in here. One would expect the government to switch it up. How many houses are getting cable television nowadays?"

Moreno shrugged.

"Let's cut the pretense," I demanded. "I know what you do. You know I know what you do. So far, I have done nothing to help the DEA toss you behind bars."

Scar groaned behind me.

I continued, "I can't find a lot of information about the Soria Cartel, except that they seem to dominate the coast of Texas, Louisiana, and north toward Kentucky. It seems like a bigger sales region than it's purported you have."

"Some of that is debatable," he claimed. "Chase, you are a fountain of surprises. What interest do you have in the Sorias? That is a family with no recompense. No remorse. You would do well to stay out of bed with such people."

"I have no intention of getting in bed with them."

Moreno's right eyebrow lifted.

"What I want is someone to tell me," I told him as I leaned forward, "where I can find them."

Moreno cocked his head quizzically. "You want to find the Soria Cartel?"

I nodded.

"For what purpose?" he asked.

"I have every intention of crushing them from the top down."

Moreno's head flew back in laughter. I noticed Scar didn't join in on Julio's mirth. Esteban Velasquez was a man that didn't mince words. He was one of the few men I'd come up against who gave me pause. Many men are killers, but few are truly capable. Scar was one of those. If he wanted to go against the Soria Cartel alone, he'd do it. Just as I recognized it in him, he knew I was serious.

"How do you plan to do that?" Moreno asked after he finished reveling in what he considered a joke.

"Let's be honest," I commented. "If I wanted to decimate your organization, I simply have to start by killing both of you."

Scar tensed, and I raised a hand. "I have no intentions, Esteban. But my point stands. What happens if someone killed the two of you?"

"Someone will step into those shoes," Moreno explained.

"Then I kill them."

"How many will you kill?" he asked.

"How many does it take for the Soria clan to slide into oblivion?"

"Chase, it would be suicidal," he told me. "Don't you agree, Esteban?"

"He's something," the enforcer agreed.

"So be it," I conceded. "I might not come out of this alive. But you have seen what I'm capable of, Julio. How many will I take out first?"

"Why should I take part in this?"

"If someone weakened the Soria Cartel, another might fill the void. Nature abhors a vacuum."

Moreno's eyes cut toward Scar. I followed his gaze to see Moreno's henchman nod.

"I cannot be a part of this," he told me. "War with the Sorias wouldn't be profitable right now."

"I'm not asking you to tag along," I explained. "Just tell me who the leaders are and where they hang their hats."

"Arturo Soria," Moreno answered. "He runs the family. *Con sus hijos.* Esteban, how many children does Soria have?"

"Four. Three sons and a daughter."

"Do they all run the cartel?" I asked.

Moreno shrugged. "Who is to say? Certainly, the sons will play a part. I cannot say about the daughter."

After a moment, he asked, "Would it matter?"

I inhaled deeply. "Yes," I finally replied. "I'm not killing anyone that's not involved."

"Even a woman? That doesn't seem like the All-American Hero."

My lip curled. "I'm not a hero."

Moreno smiled. "Arturo has a house in Alvarado. Near the water."

"Ever been there?" I asked, glancing between the two men.

"Ha, never," Moreno answered, chuckling. "We may not be at war, but Arturo would take any opportunity to remove me."

"You don't feel the same way?" I asked.

"It seems I don't need to, does it?"

I shrugged.

"Tell me, Chase," he questioned. "What takes you up against the Sorias?"

"They killed me."

24

The diner door jangled as it opened, pulling on the string of bells. I poked at the scrambled eggs as I considered my options.

My funds were running low. At least my immediate funds. I had a few thousand dollars of cash stashed on *Carina*, plus a fat account in a bank in Grand Cayman. Unfortunately, the few thousand I had on my person was down to less than $300.

"You're easy to find," Scar commented as he slid into the booth across from me.

"I figured I didn't need to go far."

"Gordon, you seem too emotional," he mentioned as he folded his hands.

"What makes you say that?" I asked.

"When we first met," he began, "you intended to battle us over your friend. A man you hadn't seen in years."

"He was still a friend."

"Friend," Velasquez spat the word out like an orange seed. "What does that matter?"

"It matters a great deal," I told him. "We were like family."

"But you weren't family. Now, you want to go to war with the Sorias. Why?"

"They killed someone I liked."

"A woman?" he asked, piqued by curiosity.

"Yes, but that's inconsequential."

"A lover?" Scar dug deeper as he tried to delve into my psyche.

"Not really," I told him. "Once, but that's not it. I saved her life, and it is my fault she's dead."

"Your fault?" the man questioned.

"I messed up. Walked right into a trap."

Scar nodded. "You can't kill yourself, so you kill those that actually killed her."

"Yes," I agreed. "Something like that."

The enforcer leaned back in the booth and looked at me. "Or maybe you can't kill yourself, so you let those that killed her do it for you?"

"I'm not suicidal," I responded blatantly.

He put both hands in the air. "You are a logical man, Gordon. I know how you think. This is not logical.

Where is your friend? The sheriff? Why aren't you taking him along to watch your–how do you say it? 'Your six?'"

"Jay? It's not his fight."

Velasquez cocked his head. "But it's yours? Because you saved this woman's life? Or because you got her killed?"

"Either answer works," I told him.

"Your friend would agree with you?" he asked.

I stared at him for a few seconds. No, Jay would try to talk me out of it. If that didn't work, he'd be loading up a go-bag to tag along. I couldn't let him do that.

Why not?

The answer wasn't what Scar said. I wasn't looking to die on this mission. I had to think of Allie's sister. She was still in danger. If I removed the threat, she'd be safe.

What would that matter, though? She's never going to wake up. Even if her husband suffocated her tomorrow, would it make her life worse? Probably the opposite.

"The thing is, I need to do this because no one else will," I finally told Velasquez. "Soria will go on killing people. Clark will go on unscathed after destroying an entire family. Someone has to stop it."

"That someone is you?" he asked.

"No one else is stepping up," I explained.

Esteban Velasquez grunted as he leaned forward. The waitress walked toward us, locking eyes with him. He shifted his eyes in a way that steered her away from the table without a word.

"Mr. Moreno can't offer any more assistance, other than what he told you," he explained.

I nodded. "I didn't expect it. What he gave me was plenty."

"If it wouldn't attract the attention to Mr. Moreno, I'd be willing to go with you."

My head turned up. I imagine my face conveyed a degree of shock. Scar and I were antagonistic allies at best. For him to make such an offer was out of character. Perhaps he really distrusted my motives. If I didn't think he'd stab me in the back if it suited him, I'd think the man might have developed some affection for me.

"I understand how you feel," the man told me. "The Sorias have no dignity."

"You think what they did was wrong?" I asked, dumbfounded.

He shook his head, dismissing any doubts I suddenly developed about his character. "No, you misunderstand. It's business. Sometimes it's ugly. However, they didn't come straight for you. I know the girl meant something, but in my business, it's just a girl. Nothing personal."

"If it were your wife or daughter?" I asked, without even knowing what kind of family he had.

"Were she mine?" he pondered. "I'd be ready to kill them all."

I shrugged.

"I understand, Gordon. But it will not be easy."

He reached into his jacket and pulled out an iPad. With the stroke of two fingers, he opened the screen and turned the screen to face me. A satellite image appeared. It was a coast-line. Scar stretched the image until a house with a red-tiled roof became clear. It was difficult to judge the actual size, but it looked large, even by South Florida standards.

"Arturo Soria's *casa*," Velasquez explained. "He has thirty acres from this road to the ocean."

"How secured is it?" I asked, examining the plot of land on the screen.

His eyes cut up from the iPad as if to scold me for a moronic question.

"Do you know numbers?" I asked, clarifying my thought.

"There are at least 20 men on the plantation at any time," Scar responded. He motioned over an area, saying, "Most patrol this area between the house and the gate." His finger touched what appeared to be a drive leading off the dirt road.

"20?"

"That does not include the family," he pointed out.

"Are they in the main house?"

Scar nodded. "This building is for the men." He touched a smaller white building a few hundred feet south of the primary structure.

I examined the image. There were six structures on the Soria property. The main house, the other house for the guards, a barn near the water with an attached fenced pasture, a shed, a small building just a few feet from the house, and a garage. Other than the buildings, there was little cover on the grounds. Most of the vegetation was no taller than scrub grass. A couple of yucca trees seemed to be scattered about the grounds, but none offered much cover.

"I guess they have that road pretty well locked down," I noted. "Is there anything else along that route?"

"No place a *gringo* wouldn't stand out," he suggested with a curled lip.

"What's the water approach like?" I asked.

The enforcer shrugged. He didn't strike me as the type to engage in any aquatic sports, much less swimming through the dark. Besides, a man as brazen as Scar would walk through the front gate with an army, gunning down every Soria in his path. He'd get the job done, but the body count on both sides would be high.

One thing I remember a drill instructor screaming at me was the direct approach was rarely the most tactical. "War ain't a fair game where both sides take turns," he explained in a loud, harsh, drill sergeant tone.

I leaned over the screen. The coastline appeared to be mostly rocks. A small stretch of sand was carved out just east of the house. It appeared either to be man-made or Soria chose the property for the seclusion. Rocks bordered the north and south sides of the private beach. The color of the water grew dark on both sides as well. The rocks must protrude into the sea while the sandy bottom in front of the beach extended out a distance. My uneducated opinion was the cut in the rocks was natural, or at least made long before Arturo Soria was around, to allow the buildup of sand.

If I were responsible for stationing guards, I'd focus my attention on the beach. Especially with limited resources. The rocks would be nearly impossible to cross. Anyone who attempted to climb through the jagged rocks with the surging surf would be ground up like old meat in a grinder.

Of course, just because something is difficult, it doesn't make it impossible.

If the water were deep enough, one could approach underwater, coming up between a few of the bigger formations. The risk of being pummeled was still high, but at least there was some protection. The dangerous part would be avoided by staying below the surface. Well, the most dangerous part. Riptides and currents through underwater openings might suck a body through an opening too small to get out.

"You plan to come in from the sea?" he asked incredulously. "That would be...difficult."

My finger traced a line along the water. "If I come in with a boat here, I can drop in and come ashore underwater."

I explained the bare bones of my initial plan. Scar's face remained mostly stoic, however the minuscule emotion in his eyes betrayed him. They seemed filled with shock and fear.

"It's dangerous," I commented.

"I don't think it would be my tactic," he admitted. "I would suspect there to be someone watching the beach."

"Possibly," I remarked. "I'll deal with it."

Scar gave me an approving glance. "When you get down to Mexico, call this number. He'll get you whatever equipment you need."

"Thanks, Esteban. I owe you." My face winced when I said that. It was a dangerous thing to owe favors to men like Esteban Velasquez and Julio Moreno.

The enforcer bowed his head reverently before standing to leave me alone in the booth with my cold eggs.

25

S ix weeks and a day passed since I died.

I'd stayed off the radar, and except for Julio Moreno and Esteban Velasquez, I hadn't connected with anyone.

The moon waned over the water with only a thin smile. Barely enough light to reflect off the water. There were no city lights to drown out the stars off the coast of Alvarado. Instead, trails of stars sparkled across the black night.

The eight-foot inflatable boat rocked as the waves pushed past it toward the shore. I floated half a mile from shore. Based on the charts I'd examined, the depth here reached only around 50 feet. The tiny dingy fought for every inch as I rowed it out. The journey took me most of the evening. Now, I had three and a half hours until dawn. It was the best time to make an incursion into an armed compound. By the time I reached shore, it would be almost four in the morning. Those on the night shift would be tiring. Morning was close, and the end of the shift was in sight, and if the night had been quiet, complacency will have set in.

My biggest problem with the small boat was fitting the gear I needed. A large blue zippered bag contained the scuba gear. Another waterproof bag carried a Trejo Modelo 2, two Glock 9 mm pistols, and several extra clips for everything. All the needed equipment filled the little inflatable vessel to the brim.

I borrowed both the boat and the dive equipment from a Sea Ray docked a hundred miles south of here. Once I got back to *Carina*, I'd send a couple of thousand anonymously to ease the owner's loss. Scar arranged the weapons through a contact in the Yucatan. After all, he'd done, I was going to have to add him to my Christmas list.

I strapped an eight-inch dive knife to my calf. The blade was razor sharp, and I marveled at how its owner kept it in such pristine condition. Once I donned my fins and mask, I slid my arms into the buoyancy compensator with the cylinder of air strapped to the back. I'd considered leaving the BC and swimming in with just the tank, but if I had any issues, I might want the inflatable vest to keep me on top of the water. Better safe than sorry.

Once I was fully decked out in my gear, I pulled the strap of the waterproof bag over my neck. It took several tries to get most of the air out of the bag. The last thing I wanted was a giant balloon carrying me to the surface before I was ready. Or worse, not letting me get down deep enough.

As I rolled off the edge of the dingy, my back hit the water first. The sea-water was icy without a wetsuit. The initial shock passed through me quickly, and my body adjusted to the temperature.

My right hand unsheathed my knife, and I raked the edge along the bottom of both edges of the boat, releasing the air in two high-pitched whistles. If the dinghy accidentally made it to shore, it might alert the guards. Likewise, if dawn came, and some observant eyes caught sight of a boat off-shore, an alarm might sound, making my job more difficult.

By the time I began letting the air out of my BC, the water spilled over the deflated gunwales of the boat and dragged it a few inches under the surface. The bubbles expelled from the regulator floated above me as I sank through the darkness.

Night diving is often an eerie experience. During the day, the visibility is usually clear, and in these waters, I should be able to see at least 100 feet. At night, there is nothing to be seen. I had a flashlight dangling from my wrist. The beam of light only illuminated a small tunnel, and the worries of what is on the edge of the light can be nerve-wracking, especially when one considers that the scary things tend to come out at night.

I only intended to use the light sparingly. It was unlikely it would be visible from the shore, but when I reached shallower waters, I was going to err on the side of caution.

Glow-in-the-dark indicators allowed me to read the depth and air gauges. A compass was strapped to the back of the depth gauge. I checked my heading, and once I was pointed west, I kicked my fins. The light bobbed around the bottom. Crabs scurried under rocks as the beam passed over them. A few fish moved close to the beam, curiosity drawing them closer.

Just at the edge of my light, a silver flash shot across my path. I paused, waiting to see if it returned. Several seconds passed before the thin body of a young barracuda crept into the shadows. I watched the toothy grin of the fish as it hung on the edge of the darkness. A school of ballyhoo swarmed through the light, picking off nearly microscopic swimmers attracted to the light. The barracuda fired out of the dark, scooping mouthfuls of the ballyhoos before vanishing into the black again.

Barracuda can be dangerous, but they don't go after things bigger than they are. That doesn't mean in the dark, this guy might mistake a flash of skin as a fish. I moved along the bottom with some increased speed.

If he was the biggest predator out here right now, I felt safe.

The problem was, I didn't know if he was the biggest one. The key was to remind myself I was a Marine, so in all likelihood, I was the biggest predator here.

Of course, try explaining that to a shark.

I kept my focus on the sand ahead of me. Even in the daylight, it's a challenge to judge distance underwater. In the dark, I did not know how far I'd swam. My depth gauge told me I was at 42 feet down. The contour of ocean floor was climbing, and I would cut my light around 20 feet. My last leg would be in the pitch black.

When I'm underwater, I find this calming peace. The kind of serenity most people meditate to achieve. To me, the solitude combined with weightlessness and an occasional fish calms my anxiety.

Several schools of small fish crossed my beam, but the lurking barracuda stayed clear. More jagged rocks began making appearances along the seafloor. I was in 25 feet of water now. My heading was still on target. If I followed the imaginary line, I should come up between two rocky faces. The local tide tables reported low tide to be around 8:50 in the morning, which meant the tide was currently dropping. Hopefully, between the dropping tide and calm weather, the water wouldn't be churning too strong there.

It's a little like hoping the shark that's attacking you isn't too big. Either way, a chunk was coming out of your skin. It's just about how bad it would be.

The beam of light cut out, leaving me in pure black. I assumed the barracuda was still nearby, and his vision was much better than mine. I hoped he was full on ballyhoos now.

The only glow I could see came from my compass and depth gauge. I was at 15 feet, but my heading held. My fingers would scrape across the bottom every few seconds to make sure I wasn't drifting toward the surface.

A full moon would have been nice about now. I could use the glow to orient myself, but once I was on shore, it would be more of an issue. No, I just kept moving forward until I bumped into a solid surface. My mask struck first, bouncing off the rock wall. I still couldn't see anything.

My hand shielded the flashlight's lens as I turned it on. The red glow of the light shining through my flesh cast a blood red aura in the water. I breathed a sigh of relief that the barracuda wasn't sitting inches away from my face. Even the toughest badass might have wet himself with a shock like that.

The rock barrier curved upward, creating a small alcove under the water. I double-checked my depth—14 feet.

My left arm raised over my head as I inflated my BC. The inflatable vest carried me toward the surface. As I moved upward, the rock narrowed around me. The closer I got to the surface, the more turbulent the water became as it pushed off each side of the wall. The BC bounced me off the rock on one side and into the rock on the other.

My head broke through the surface. My hands extended to keep me from slamming too hard into any one side. The face of the wall was covered in sharp edges. Plenty of handholds, but they were all razor-sharp.

I kept one hand up to shield my body from the walls while I released the buckles on my BC. In one fluid motion, I slid out of the vest and turned it to protect me. My hand reached down and pulled the strap off my left fin, letting it fall into the abyss below. My left toes slipped the other fin free.

With my feet free, I pushed toward one side of the alcove. The BC continued to buffer me from the jagged edges as I stretched up and found a handhold. My right arm lifted me up, and I pressed my feet against the wall until the toes on my right foot found a perch. Once my arms braced me, I began my ascent. Initially, the waves pulsed against me, and it took the strength of all four appendages to keep the force from pulling me off the wall or scraping me against it. However, as the water receded for a second,

I used the respite to scale up a few feet before bracing for the next wave surge. Within a couple of minutes, I was completely out of the water.

The climb was only 20 or so feet. Once I wasn't fighting the ocean, it grew easier. I could feel the salt water burning the cuts I'd sustained on the wall. They'd have to wait for any kind of evaluation and care. For now, I'd let the blood drip into the water below. When I crested the top, I stared across the scrub brush toward the white house in the distance. The house wasn't dark. I imagined there were few times the lights were all off. The upstairs windows were black, but several on the first floor let out the light from inside. It was a common mistake. The alert guards inside would have a hard time seeing out the windows if the interior rooms were lighted. It was complacency, something that gets people killed regularly.

It was something I was counting on.

Staying low on the rocks, I unrolled the waterproof bag. Besides the guns and ammunition, the bag held a dry set of dark clothes—a black shirt and combat pants. Wrapped in the clothes, a pair of running shoes were folded up. I'd picked them up in a flea market on the side of the road, along with half a can of red spray paint. There wasn't any black, but the dark red would work just as well out here. The now red shoes slipped onto my feet once I'd dressed.

The extra clips found homes in the different pockets of the combat pants, and I ensured the guns were loaded before I pushed up to my knees.

My eyes scanned across the compound for several minutes until I located the sentries making their rounds. There were two sets outside. Four guards total. From where I sat, I watched one set engaged in conversation against a fence. They stood in the same place, talking, for over five minutes before meandering along a lighted footpath.

Complacency.

It was time for me to go.

Hell was about to be unleashed.

26

With no cover, I stayed low to the ground as I maneuvered around the scrub brush. A split wood fence ran along one side of the compound. A small barn was set back from the fence. Two Appaloosa mares stood motionless in the field. I slid between the fence to use the posts as cover. It wouldn't hide my body, but in the dark the pattern might hide my movement from a sentry's peripheral vision.

As I moved along the pasture line, I saw a shape in front of the house. A familiar helicopter sat on Arturo Soria's front lawn. The same chopper I pulled David Royce out of on Swan Island.

Scar warned there would be at least 20 men on the property. Most should be asleep in their beds, and if I didn't want them to come out with their guns blazing, I needed to keep things quiet for the time being.

Once the shooting started, it was going to make finishing the job more difficult.

The two men I'd watched talking near the fence line were making their way toward me again. It had taken them nearly 20 minutes to walk the path around the property. With the dive knife in my hand, I crouched lower to the ground and stayed perfectly still.

One man let out a laugh as the other said something in Spanish. I tightened my grip on the blade and waited. The two continued to talk. One slowed as he came near the wooden fence, and he pulled a pack of cigarettes from his pocket. A familiar clicking from a lighter echoed across the pasture.

The man leaned his back against the fence only ten feet from my position. A sweet smell of tobacco crawled across the ground.

His friend shifted on his feet as his compatriot enjoyed his vice. He made a comment that sounded like he was rushing his partner. The smoker seemed to wave off whatever was said.

When the man put the cigarette to his lips, I watched the end glow in the darkness as he inhaled. I sprang out of my crouch and drove the blade of my dive knife into the smoker's neck. The other man turned as I came over the fence. He kept his gun holstered on his side, and before he could pull the weapon, I collided with him.

My weight buckled the man's knees as I hit him. When we hit the ground, I rolled to my feet and charged the guard as he tried to stand up and get his weapon. My first blow struck his larynx. Instinct sent both of his hands toward his throat as he gasped for air. My second blow was a fist that landed just below his sternum. Any air he had in his lungs spewed out as the man fell backward.

I landed on top of him, driving my right knee into his ribs. The crack was inaudible, but I felt the pressure give way under my weight. My right fist hammered into his face as he tried to lift his head. His skull bounced off the ground once before lolling to the right. He was still breathing, but unconscious. I glanced at his smoking buddy, who had slid lifeless down the fence with the hilt of my knife protruding from the side of his neck.

After taking both men's guns, I broke the fingers of the guard lying on the ground. I didn't feel right about killing him while he was out, but if he woke up, I wasn't keen on him being able to shoot at me, either. His hand would heal.

The blade of my dive knife made a squishing sound as I pulled it free. I wiped the blade clean on the man's clothes before sheathing it.

Neither man carried a radio, which meant there wasn't someone waiting for a regular report. Given the lackadaisical approach to sentry rounds, that made perfect sense. Both men carried Smith and Wesson .45s. I slipped one under the waistband at the small of my back, and I pulled the magazine from the other. The emptied weapon landed in the grass.

I peered across the yard. No one seemed to be alerted. There was no alarm being sounded.

As I approached the house, the area had more lights. So far, my presence was undetected, and no one was looking. I moved along the footpath toward the house. My right hand hung at my side, holding the Trejo. With a Glock holstered on each hip, I looked like a post-apocalyptic gunslinger as I moved toward the house.

The Trejo held 11 rounds. I wanted to save the shooting until I was inside the house. The walls of both the main house and the guards' sleeping quarters might muffle the sound enough to slow the response time.

Of course, I had to get inside first.

On the front porch of the main house stood two guards. The way they stood differed from the two I'd just dispatched. There was a sense of importance to their duties. It might be why they had the post on the porch.

The house was a typical Spanish style, covered with stucco and rounded edges. Every window was arched. Columns trimmed the porch. Lights on the corners of the house transformed the night into day. Installed just above the first level, they did not fill the upstairs bedrooms with light at night.

As I studied the house, I found the hole in their defense. The southeast corner didn't have lights on it. It was a courtesy for the guards' quarters, which sat just off that side. They didn't want to keep the men awake with bright lights. Besides, who is going to come past the guardhouse?

The downside to the bright lights for the men on the porch is their eyes get adjusted to them. Everything outside of the light remained hidden. All I needed to do was skirt the edge of the light, and the two men could almost stare directly at me without seeing me.

When I reached the darkened corner, I scampered close to the ground like one of those crabs I passed earlier, staying low to the ground and sticking to the shadows. Once I reached the house, I examined the outside. The stucco, while textured, left few handholds for climbing.

I still had almost two and a half hours till sunrise. Plenty of time.

My best point of entry was to use the first-floor window. The only issue was the light inside was on. Was someone in there, or did they simply leave the room without turning off the light?

My hand reached up and tested the window. It was the kind that swung open so the Sorias could enjoy the ocean air. When I pulled the pane, the metal clicked as the latch prevented it from opening. I took a step back to get a better look. No one came to the window, but I might not have made that much noise. A strong breeze off the water could rattle the windows.

I pulled my knife free and gently tapped the window. Rhythmic enough to draw curiosity. A few seconds passed with no response. I tried again, harder.

A shadow moved, and I waited. Two feet above where I crouched, a face appeared. The man had a thick mustache and beady eyes. He pressed his face against the glass, trying to see out.

I turned the blade in my hand and watched. As he lifted his hand to shield the light, I swung my hand over my head. The blade shattered the glass and drove into his right eye. Glass sliced my knuckles, and I wished I'd protected them. Hell, if I'd just given that a second thought.

Too late. I reached through the broken window and flipped the latch. The dead guard's weight pushed the swinging panes open, and I pulled him through the opening. I waited for a response. The breaking glass sounded loud to me, but with the wind and waves in the distance, it seemed to be swallowed up.

My head peered over the sill. The room was empty. I squatted down and checked the man. He had another .45 and a switchblade. I kept the blade and left the gun. I was already carrying more firearms than I had hands.

Another quick look inside showed the room still empty. I tossed my Trejo through the window before hoisting my body over the sill.

The room was a parlor. A small bar was built into the corner with several bottles of tequila and whiskey. At the center of the room, a yellow sofa with matching chairs on either side sat in a U shape. An ornate coffee table sat between the seats with intricate carvings of mermaids and fish. Over the mantle of the fireplace, a painting hung. Even a neophyte like myself recognized the style of Frida Kahlo. It was the centerpiece so that all of Arturo Soria's guests knew he had it. A reminder to all that Soria could have anything.

I moved toward the arched opening that led to the darkened foyer. I gripped the Trejo in my right hand and the dive knife in my left. As I rounded the corner to the foyer, I saw a dark corridor leading to the back of the house. At the end of the hall, a door opened on a kitchen. The light spilled out of the doorway. On either side of the hall were two closed doors.

I took two steps down the tiled corridor when a toilet flushed behind me. The door on the left side of the hall opened as I twisted around. A short, stubby man stepped out as he cinched his belt. He froze, locking eyes with me in surprise.

Before he reacted, the Trejo came up and spit four rounds into his chest. The reports from the Trejo were somewhat quiet. They sounded like a baseball card stuck in the wheels of a bicycle. Bd-bd-bd-bd. The crash of the man's body falling against the wall made more racket than the gun. He dragged a framed picture off the wall that shattered when it hit the floor.

"*¿Estás bien?*" a voice called from the kitchen.

I turned back as a figure filled the illuminated doorway. The barrel of the little machine pistol came up. Bd-Bd-bd. As the figure fell, I charged toward the kitchen. The front door slammed open as the two men on the porch pushed through to investigate.

I stepped over the body in the kitchen, sweeping the Trejo around as I verified the room was empty.

"*En la cocina.*"

Gun-fire erupted down the hallway. My back pressed against the wall as the bullets slammed into the counters across from me. Guess my stealthy assault was over. I dropped to one knee, extended the Trejo around the door jamb a foot from the floor and fired.

Bd-bd-bd-bd.

The gun clicked after the last round fired. My hand jerked back, shed the empty magaizine, and slapped in a new one. I spewed all eleven rounds down the hallway.

Bd-bd-bd-bd-bd-bd-bd-bd-bd-bd-bd.

A muffled thud sounded like one of the gunmen fell to the floor. Two more shots struck a stack of copper pots on the counter, sending them scattering to the floor in a clang. On my hands and knees, I crawled across the kitchen to the eight-burner range.

The gunman fired through the door, blindly. His shots struck the counter six feet to my left. My foot pushed against the counter as I heaved the heavy stove away from the wall. The metal legs screeched as they dragged across the kitchen floor. I twisted and fired several rounds toward the door. I wouldn't hit anything, but I wanted the man on the other end of the hallway to stay down.

Between shooting, I pulled the dive knife free and reached behind the stove. The edge of the blade sliced through the yellow gas line. A slight whistle came from behind the appliance as the natural gas seeped through the opening. With haste, I scampered back to the door and fired the rest of the magazine down the hall.

I had one more magazine for the Trejo. After the next barrage of shots, I heard the clatter as the shooter released the empty magazine to the floor. Twisting around, the corner, I fired.

Bd-bd-bd-bd-bd-bd-bd-bd-bd-bd-bd.

The gunman was popping out for a shot when the Trejo unloaded into him. He jerked violently as at least nine of the eleven rounds riddled his body.

I dropped the Trejo to the kitchen floor, pulled both Glocks from the holsters on my hips and moved back down the corridor.

27

Footsteps overhead pounded through the ceiling. The gunfire woke up the family. I stalked into the foyer and slammed the front door. There were two dead-bolts on the solid oak door. My fingers twisted both, securing the door. It wouldn't stop the cavalry, but it might slow them down. I guessed there were at least two other entry points, but I didn't take the time to search for them.

I moved toward the stairs on the west side of the foyer. The builder curved the steps to flow around the room to a landing overlooking the front door. As I climbed, a door at the top of the landing opened. A 30-something man came through the opening. The gunfire roused him from the bed, and donning a pair of sweatpants, he charged downstairs to investigate the ruckus. He held a chrome Colt .45 revolver up, ready for action.

Instinct said this was one of the Soria boys. The rashness with which he ran into action told me he had something to prove. If he was the youngest, he would definitely be the angriest. While I could psychoanalyze him all day, I let the brief inference slip through my mind as I fired the left Glock. The round caught him center mass, stopping his heart immediately. The Colt clattered down the steps.

It was a nice weapon. I considered taking it, but the revolver only held six rounds. While they'd punch a hole through whatever I shot, I wanted quantity right now.

High-pitched screams in Spanish flooded through the open door. The quandary of my assault was about to arrive.

Most of the time, a battle is never as fast-paced as the movies play it out. Guns don't have unlimited ammo, so even the most well-armed combatant reaches a point when he has to conserve his supplies. Most military operations count on a quick resolution. Get in, shoot everyone, get out—all before you run out of ammo. Those ops are standard. They involve a team of six to ten highly trained soldiers. Even those actions might seem fast for the civilian watching, but it's not. A successful action is methodical, meaning each advance in the battle results from careful consideration.

The action slows even more when there is only one insurgent. Until now, I was pushing forward. Clear the perimeter. Clear the bottom floor. Move to the stairs.

However, from here, everything changed. The Soria family was on the other side of the door. That included Arturo and his remaining sons and only daughter. Not to mention their spouses and children.

The thing with war is knowing who the enemy is. Hollywood defines the bad guy with all the right tropes. In reality, they aren't so easy to define. Some days, it's the six-year-old kid with enough C4 strapped to his chest to take out a city block. Other times, the demure woman has a gun in her hand. Those moments are the ones that happen too fast in battle. The split-second decision of "is this an enemy or a by-stander." Can they live or die?

Arturo Soria was the bad guy. It's sexist, but also fair to assume that his sons have a hand in the day-to-day operations. But their wives? The children? The culture is patriarchal. Does that mean I can assume there's no threat? Every mother, wife, and daughter has a vested interest in their family.

The question remains—who do I shoot?

Philosophizing aside, I pulled the stairwell door open. Three gunshots splintered the frame from down the hall.

The front door rattled below as off-duty guards charged toward the fight. The deadbolts held as two or three men attempted to throw their shoulders against the oak door.

I turned back to the dark hallway. My left hand raised the Glock and fired three shots in a sweeping pattern. After pulling the trigger the third time, I took advantage of the cover fire to turn on the light switch. The overhead light illuminated the corridor. Three doors were spaced on both walls of the hall. Two hung open, with shadows in the doorway.

The light in the second to last door on the right shifted. I pulled back as a boom echoed down the hall. My left foot pivoted as I fired repeatedly down the hall before I charged down.

I aimed each shot at the two opened doors. As I pulled the trigger, the shooters should instinctively pull back.

In a perfect world, at least.

I charged down the hall, firing two more shots. The corridor echoed the gunfire, masking the sound of my feet as they ran along the carpeted floor. As I twisted into the open door, a figure lurched back in the black. It didn't matter; I sacked him. We slammed into a wall. Picture frames rattled as they fell off their nails and clattered to the floor. A female screamed a few feet from me.

The man in the dark wasn't expecting the tackle. His feet buckled under the pressure, and I came down on top of him. His grip on his gun tightened as the silhouette of it swung toward my head. My left arm came down on his forearm, driving his weapon to the floor.

My right hand swung the Glock out like a hammer. The impact of metal on flesh gave a soft, gooshy thunk sound. A repeated blow elicited a crack as bone broke under the blow. Underneath me, the man went limp, and I pushed up to my feet.

For a second, the upstairs was quiet. The other shooter was trying to decipher what was happening. Rapid sobbing came from where the woman had screamed only seconds earlier. I moved to the door and found the light switch.

A half-naked woman sat on the California king-sized bed against the back wall. The down comforter draped across her, but she'd pulled it up to cover half her face as if it would protect her. Two bare legs stretched from the bottom of the blanket. Her dark brown eyes teared as she trembled.

Behind her, a double window stretched from the floor to the ceiling. One side was ajar, letting the ocean breeze fill the room. In roughly an hour, the sunrise would offer itself to make the perfect view.

On the floor, the man was unconscious. Blood matted the dark black hair to the left side of his skull. The blow from the Glock fractured his skull. His chest moved up and down, but he wasn't joining the fight anytime soon.

The weapon he dropped was another silver Colt .45–almost identical to the one the first Soria dropped on the stairwell.

"Salvatore?" a voice cried from down the hallway.

I glanced at the man on the floor, guessing he was Salvatore.

"*Está en el cuarto de Salvatore,*" the same voice called.

An explosion boomed from below. A shotgun blast was followed by a crack of wood as the front door slammed open.

Reinforcements.

"*¡Mátenlo!*"

"*¡Arriba!*" someone below shouted.

I turned to look at the frightened woman, who was now frozen. Her glassy eyes stared at me as she waited. I reloaded the two Glocks with fresh magazines. I had two more full s left in my pocket.

"*¿Emesta, estás bien?*"

The woman's eyes shifted. It was the only bit of Spanish I understood. The man down the hallway was calling for her, asking her if she was okay. I raised a finger to my lips. She didn't move.

I wasn't sure what the gamble was. Was this the daughter? Or was Salvatore the son, making Emesta the wife or girlfriend? The commanding tone down the hallway sounded older. I guessed the voice belonged to Arturo. How far would he stick his neck out for this Emesta?

"Arturo Soria!" I called out.

The upstairs hallway was quiet. Even the clamoring up the stairwell stopped when I shouted.

"Who are you?" the old voice responded.

I ignored the question. There was no point in telling the cartel who I was. It didn't matter to me if Arturo Soria knew he never killed Chase Gordon. My ego didn't need to see him realize his failure. Not that the satisfaction wouldn't hit the spot, but logic dictates that no matter how this night ends, there would still be Sorias looking for vengeance. The idea of cutting off the head of a serpent works great when dealing with an actual snake. But in the real world, it's more like a chimera. Cut off one head, and another appears.

"Salvatore can't talk now," I shot back, "but Emesta is safe and sound."

"What do you want?" he asked.

"I want you," I replied. "Step into the hallway."

A woman shouted something down the hallway. Soria responded in mumbled Spanish.

"You will not survive," he finally shouted at me.

"Neither will Emesta, if you don't come down here."

A rapid fire of Spanish came quickly, and I guessed the meaning either questioned my parentage or instructed me to violate myself.

"Bien," he called. "I'm coming."

Emesta pulled her knees up and muttered something under her breath. It sounded like a prayer.

The house was still. I imagined a small troop standing at the door of the stairwell. At least Arturo was at the other end of the hallway. There should be at least one other son, assuming that Salvatore and the one on the stairwell were Sorias. Don't discount the women. While the cartel culture doesn't put a lot of stock in women, it is moronic to ignore them. Women are often deadlier than men.

The floor in the hallway creaked as Arturo made his way slowly toward me.

How many men had I encountered so far? Six? Seven?

Both Glocks raised up. Soria's footsteps were slow. Deliberate.

How do you plan to get out of here, Gordon?

Even if I killed Arturo, there were at least ten, maybe 15, men waiting to gun me down.

Scar called me suicidal. I didn't think I was, but I found myself pinned in by a small army.

"*¡Mátenlos!*" Arturo screamed.

Emesta's eyes widened as the hallway erupted with pounding feet. Instinct screamed, "Take cover!" I bolted away from the wall as the first gunshots bellowed through the house.

With a dive, I soared over the corner of the bed as Emesta howled.

There's an indescribable sound that once a person heard it, they recognize instantly. The sound of a body being riddled with bullets. I didn't need to look to see Emesta as she slumped back. The down comforter made for little defense.

I fired blindly over the mattress at the door as gunfire peppered the bed.

A huff of air rushed through the house, followed by a boom that shook the house. When the kitchen exploded, it wasn't like the movies. The initial blast ignited the gas in the air. It vibrated the walls and shattered some windows, but the structure didn't erupt.

It was, however, enough to draw panic to the men in the hallway. All I needed was a second, as I sprang over the bloodied corpse of Emesta. My shoulder crashed through the half-opened window frame as I fell over the wrought-iron railing into the dark night.

28

The fall was about 15 feet, but I didn't measure it on the way down. Instead, I curled in a ball, so I could land in a roll. Most injuries resulting from short falls like that come from awkward landing. A flailing arm might break. An attempt to land on one's feet can cause a snapped ankle. The best course is to hit the ground with the most bounce. So, to speak. Therefore, I cannon-balled it, landing on the left side of my back. I tumbled across the ground as rocks and sticks ripped my skin open.

When the rolling stopped, I bounded to my feet. A quick self-evaluation determined no bones broke in the fall. Screams and shouts rolled out of the house. Smoke billowed up behind an orange glow. Flames were flickering out the kitchen window. While the initial explosion resulted in minimal damage, the leaking gas lines fueled the flames. No amount of water was going to extinguish it until they cut the gas supply.

I started running toward the fence-line and crawled into the pasture. From the field, I watched as the remaining members of the household ran out of the burning house. Chaos ran rampant around the house. Men were shouting and pointing. Three women huddled with four armed men shielding them. The sentries swept pistols in arcs in front of them as they waited for me to attack.

It would be easy to slip back to the rocks and vanish into the ocean. My BC might still be sloshing around the alcove in the rock wall.

I tried to count the men on the grounds. As they moved in and out of the burning house, it was difficult to keep track of which ones were which, but I ended up getting to twelve. The one staring into the darkness with his arms crossed was Arturo. His stance and demeanor marked him as the leader. The rest offered a deference to him, recognizable even in the shadows.

He pointed toward the ocean and barked something. Six men scattered out of the light. The hunt was on, and I was the prey.

Twelve men.

I had four full clips. Each magazine held 17 rounds. If I hit what I was aiming for, I'd only need one gun.

Things aren't always so simple, though. Those men only had one target. The odds were stacked towards them.

I sprinted toward the barn. I spooked one of the horses as I ran past her. Her hooves thudded against the dirt as she bolted away. The whinny and huff she let out after he settled was a warning to me and an alert to my hunters.

Without looking back, I slipped into the dark stables. In the loft of the trussed barn, fresh cut hay must have been stacked. The Mexican heat dried the last of the moisture, leaving a faint aroma of cut grass in the air. A tiny glow of light shone through the open door and windows that allowed the breeze to cool the interior.

My back pressed against a wall, and I edged my way along slowly. I grew up in rural Arkansas, where I'd seen my fair share of barns. They had one thing in common. They were collection bins for everything on the farm. Everything from rakes to plows had sharp, pointy ends perfect for impaling someone in the dark. It wasn't advisable to run through most barns in the daylight. When it was pitch black, it was deadly.

My feet shuffled through the dust. The particles of dry dirt kicked up the air as I moved, filling my nostrils and mouth.

The first light came through the door a few seconds later. My knees bent as I lowered myself down. A beam of light swept across the barn. The man behind the light was moving too fast. Even if the spotlight passed right over me, he'd still miss me.

My eyes followed the beam as it moved, taking a mental picture of the layout. Despite my suspicions, the barn was fairly immaculate. At least for a barn. There was a ladder leading to the loft on the opposite side from me. To the rear of the barn, I noticed a door. Three stalls stood across from me. They were all empty since the horses were in the field.

A second man filled the doorway behind the light.

"*¿Míralo?*" the second man asked in a hushed voice.

Flashlight turned and whispered something I couldn't understand. I lined the first man's figure up in the sights of the 9 mm in my right hand. Two cracks sounded in the dark. Both men fell in the doorway.

I moved across the barn to the second stall, where I crouched and waited. The gunshots would bring others. Before the next shape to fill the doorway had time to shine a light, the Glock boomed again, and I watched his body twist to his left and fall.

If the six men sent out to hunt me spread out evenly, these three would be the closest. The other three would go to the cliff wall and work this way. Until the gun-shots alerted them. Now they were running toward the barn.

The horses galloped around. Their pounding hooves sounded the proximity alarm.

Three bodies in the doorway. No way was the next guy that stupid. He'd come around the back side. Most likely while another came through the front.

With a gun in each hand, I climbed up the loft ladder into the darkness. The next wave wouldn't be so fast. They were going to work their way in slowly, prodding each side to determine my location.

When I reached the loft, I slipped the Glock in my right hand into the holster on my hip. I wanted my dominant hand free as I climbed onto the trusses framing the barn. In a few seconds, I'd scaled across the open area. Free climbing in the dark was nerve-wracking. I needed to move quietly and quickly. When I reached the opposite side of the barn, I moved my feet around until I found the lip that ran around the top of the barn wall. My back hunched forward because of the pitch of the roof I pressed against.

I guessed it was a twelve-foot span between trusses. With some reluctance, I released my grip on the wooden truss and slid my feet slowly to the side. For the next few seconds, I had nothing to hold on to. If I leaned forward too far, I'd fall face first onto the floor of the barn. As I reached the next truss, the next gun man came through the back. He waited until the man on the front shined a light through the door. It was a quick flash, and the guy in the front remained out of the doorway.

The light was intended to divert my attention for a split second. If I had not perched above the action, I might have missed the one in the rear slip inside.

As long as I stayed still, there was an excellent chance they'd never spot me. My position had me nestled in the corner of the rafters. Unless they spotlighted me, I was invisible.

Through the darkness below, I had no line of sight on the man slinking around. The only light came from the house through the front door, casting a rectangular light on the ground. I watched the glowing patch for a shadow.

No one came through that door.

I counted off the seconds in my brain.

Two minutes passed.

The one man I knew was in the barn was a ghost. If he was moving, he did so in absolute silence.

Four minutes passed.

Time is relative. Four minutes on a surfboard is like a microsecond. Four minutes in a barn with a man who killed at least 12 men must feel like an eternity. He'd be getting anxious, asking the same questions. Where was I? Could I see him? All those fears would bubble up—at least they do in most men. Once it happens, he'll be desperate to find me.

Five minutes.

Another man came through the back. From my angle, I watched his shadow pass in front of the open door before melting into darkness.

After six minutes, the third man came through the front. The rectangular light on the ground grew dark for a split second as he came through the door.

By my count, there were still four men guarding the women, Arturo, and at least one son. If everyone was home.

"*¿Dónde está?*" someone asked in the darkness.

"*No sé.*"

Their patience was wearing thin.

"*Arriba.*"

"*Enciende tu lámpara.*"

A flashlight came on, illuminating the stables. One man started climbing the ladder to the hayloft, as the other two took up a firing position, aiming up. With all three illuminated, I leveled the barrel at the closest man on the ground. I tried to listen for reinforcements outside. There didn't seem to be anything.

The muzzle flash strobed in the darkness as two shots dropped the men on the ground. Their bodies fell, and the flashlight rolled away. When the beam of light cast up against the far wall, I realized my mistake. The darkness swallowed the man on the ladder.

I heard him scampering over the top of the ladder. It was the only clue I had to his location. Not enough to fire wildly in the dark.

Of course, he wasn't shooting back either. Since his back was to me as I shot his comrades, he didn't know where I was either. It was a stalemate. Only now, he'd have more patience. How long before Arturo sends more men?

I considered repositioning on the truss, climbing out over the middle of the room. However, the risk of breaking cover didn't seem worth it.

So, we waited. The silence was deafening. I held the barrel of the 9 mm up, ready to fire if I found his location.

Seconds clicked past.

Across the barn, I could hear his breathing. Rapid huffs of breath. The acoustics of the stables made it impossible to pinpoint a direction.

My attention remained focused. Fire the gun, I pleaded mentally. All I needed was the flash to direct all my fire. I might miss him, but at least I'd send him scurrying for cover. That might buy me a few minutes.

Time to decide, Gordon. Do you make a run for it, or finish it all off?

We don't run for it, I decided.

The beam of light surprised me as it swept over me from the rear of the barn. I heard no one else enter. By the time I shifted my aim toward the light, the gunfire started.

I fired two shots at the beam as a bullet struck the wood only a few inches from my hand. Instinct released my grip, but as the second volley started, I lost my footing.

My chest struck the rafter I had been standing on, both arms slammed over the top of it. The Glock jarred from my grip as I tried to hold the rafter long enough to slow my fall.

A splinter of wood drove through my palm, ripping the skin between my thumb and index finger. The shard tore from the rafter as I fell.

29

Dust billowed around me as I landed on the barn floor. Whoever shot at me dropped their light down when they saw me fall. My knees and feet pedaled and clawed in the dirt as I moved to run for cover.

The barn echoed with gunfire as they tried to target me. There was enough light from the one flashlight on the ground to see the shapes in the barn. I cut a weave through the center toward the stables. Heaving myself through the opening, I rolled in the dirt and manure.

My right hand burned and throbbed. I pulled my remaining Glock from its holster and waited. Without the benefit of light, I reached my right hand up to my teeth. They bit down on the chunk of rafter protruding through my palm. I couldn't see it, but it felt like it was three inches long and two inches wide. It was like a fraction of that, but it still rendered that hand useless for the moment.

With a grunt, I pulled the splinter through the skin. It felt like it did more damage coming out than when it initially pierced the hand.

"You cannot get away," Arturo boasted from the shadows. "You're trapped."

"How many men are you down, Artie?" I retorted.

He breathed out what sounded like a curse. "You won't see morning."

The ceiling over me creaked, and I fired six shots into the wood above me. There was a groan and a thud.

"I think that's one more," I reported.

Arturo Soria let out a howl and fired six shots at the three stalls. His rounds zinged and tore through the wood, but they weren't near me. I don't think he knew which one was my hiding place. I wasn't sure either. I just dove for cover.

The wood constructing the stalls was nailed tight against each other, however, the same care put into building the exterior walls wasn't put into the stalls. Small cracks between the planks allowed light to seep in. Dark blobs seemed to move along the cracks as someone passed between the light and the stalls.

"*En los puestos,*" Arturo told someone. I heard the metallic clink of spent shells bouncing against each other.

I rolled to the back of the stall, staying flat on my stomach. Another spit of gunfire echoed in the walls. I counted eleven or twelve shots before there was a pause. Two men firing six shooters–matching silver Colt .45s.

More clinking, followed by another barrage of gunfire.

A few rounds slammed into the earth closer to me than I would like. As soon as the volley stopped, I raised up and fired at a dark blob in a crack. Eight shots exploded from the Glock. The blob vanished, and a widened gap appeared where the slugs ripped away the edge of the two planks.

"Neto!" Arturo screamed. "No!"

I fired the last three shots in my 9 mm at a shadow, but as the gun clicked on an empty chamber, the stall door jerked open. A silhouette appeared, and a glint of silver flashed. I hurled the empty Glock at the figure. The handgun struck something. Enough to slow him as I sprang toward the figure.

My injured hand caught the barrel, jerking it to the side as he fired. The heat of the blast burned my wound, but I drove forward. My forehead slammed into Arturo's face. The two of us tumbled backward into the dirt.

"*¡Cabrón!*" the drug lord shouted.

He swung the Colt toward me, but I struck him in the throat. My hand swept against his forearm as he gasped for air. I heard the six-shooter hit the dirt, and I rolled off him to find it.

The fiend recovered and lunged at me, slamming me against the outside wall of the stall. I caught the top of the stall door and jerked it into him. The blow wasn't hard enough to hurt him, but it surprised him enough to deliver a punch to his kidneys.

I let out a howl as my injured hand hit him. The punch was ineffective, and he struck me in the nose. I felt the cartilage break. The taste of blood filled my mouth.

The older man wrapped his arms around me and hurled me across the room. Surprised, I bounced into the darkness.

"Damn," I howled as I pulled myself up. "That's some old man strength."

"Argg!" he screamed, charging me.

He was a ball of rage. There was no other way this could end. The impact of the man drove me into a wall of tools. Metal clanged as the shovels and pitchforks clattered off the wall.

I rolled away from him as he swung a shovel at me. The square blade landed flat on my back as I tried to get to my feet. In the dim light, I saw him twist it to bring the edge down like an ax toward me. My feet spun to sweep him off his feet, and the blade dug into the dirt.

As we both scrambled to our feet, I grabbed a wooden handle. My first parry blocked Arturo as he drove the shovel blade toward my head. He took another swing with more force. The flat shovel shattered the wooden handle and pushed me to the ground.

The light behind him darkened his features, and his oily black eyes burned when he pulled back to strike again. As his blow came down, I drove the splintered end of the pitchfork handle into his abdomen. The wooden stick shoved him back, and I let the wood roll in my hands until I was swinging it like a Louisville Slugger at his knees. He buckled as his right knee gave way.

Spinning the broken pitchfork in my hands, I shoved the fork tines under his ribcage and twisted. The drug lord slumped forward, letting the shovel fall to the floor. His oily black eyes turned brown as the metal spears ripped through his organs.

I held him by the fork head for several seconds. He stared into my face. Without another word, the life passed from him, and the question of who I was remained unanswered.

When I let go of the pitchfork, Arturo Soria slumped back. He laid back in the dirt staring up into the black.

I rose to my feet. There were still four men and the women. If I could count. I walked over to the flashlight on the ground. The beam swept across the barn. Three men were piled by the front door. Two men sprawled at the bottom of the ladder to the loft. Neto Soria bled into the dirt and shit next to the stalls. And Arturo.

Would the rest matter?

Not likely.

Unless I intended to kill the women too, the Sorias would rise again.

I knew I would not do that.

In which case, what good are four more bodies?

Two silver Colts lay in the dust. I picked them both up. A matching set. I glanced at the two Sorias. Each had a leather holster on his hip. Matching holsters. As I walked to Arturo, I pulled the dive knife out. The blade cut through the man's belt, and the holster came off.

I considered taking Neto's too, but it seemed too macabre. Instead, I found my Glocks, holstered them, and moved to the back of the barn.

Once I was away from the structure, I looked back at the house. Tongues of flames licked out from every window. The crowd in the front had moved off. Out here there was no local fire brigade. I counted four men with the women. They were staying vigilant until their boss returned. They'd get no fight from me.

I climbed through the fence and jogged east. The morning sky was lightening. It wouldn't be long until the first rays of sunlight seeped over the horizon. From the top of the cliff, I straightened and looked back one last time.

Then, as the waves crashed against the wall of rock and receded, I dove in.

30

The office of Banyan Freight was on Commissioners Street in an area of Toronto called the Port Lands. The three-story building was only a block from Lake Ontario. The street passed a concrete canal cut into the city to connect to the lake.

A chill was in the air this morning, a stark difference from the climate in Mexico I'd been in a few days earlier. The wind off the lake cut through my jacket, raising goosebumps on my arms. I tugged the front of the coat tighter as the weather reminded me of all the reasons I tried to remain south of Orlando.

I leaned against a brick wall across the street from the red stone building. For the last two days, I held my vigil, watching for any sign of Steven Clark. His face wasn't hard to find. Even someone as averse to the internet as I was could track down his social media.

So far, Clark hadn't shown up. The offices opened at eight in the morning. The office staff arrived between a quarter to seven and ten after eight. A few stragglers wandered in until nine. None of them were Steven Clark.

The sky was filling with heavy clouds. The city expected snow over the next few hours. I didn't want to stand out here in the snow.

The light changed from red to green, and I crossed the four lanes of traffic. When I entered the double glass doors, I found the lobby stifling warm. Immediately, I unzipped my parka.

Brass letters hung on the wall reading, "Banyan Freight" and "Moving the World For You." An older pale woman with faux auburn hair offered me a smile.

"Welcome to Banyan Freight," she greeted.

I returned her smile as I rested against her counter. "I'm here to see Steven Clark," I informed her.

Her visage shifted less than subtly. Her features must give away all her secrets.

"Mr. Clark is not here," she told me.

"Oh, that's odd. We were scheduled to meet today."

Her head cocked sideways as she asked, "Who are you with?"

I didn't answer, offering a scoff that should have told her it was none of her affair. "Why don't you let me talk to Bryan then?" I requested. Lucky I'd remembered the name Allie mentioned back on Swan Island.

The receptionist balked again. "Bryan White?" she stuttered. "He's no longer with the company."

Now, my face must have expressed confusion.

"Who did you say you were with?" she asked again.

A more direct approach might work.

"I'm Chase Gordon," I explained. "I'm acquainted with Allie Tremblay."

"Oh, Ms. Tremblay. Would you like to speak with her?"

My eyes widened. I imagined they widened like a cartoon character. "Is she available?" I questioned.

"Let me check," the woman offered, picking up the phone. She dialed a number and said, "Patrice, there's a Chase Gordon here to see Ms. Tremblay."

She listened for a second.

"Yes, I'll send him up," she responded before placing the phone in the cradle.

She turned to face me, saying, "If you'll take the elevator up to three, you should see Patrice's desk."

I nodded, unable to form a clear thought. The elevator dinged as soon as I pushed the button.

How was Allie here? It made little sense to me. She couldn't be, unless Fretsh was wrong. It could have been another woman's body found. Surely, she'd know I would worry. But it's not like Allie knew how to get in touch with me. I don't have a phone, and for the last two months, I've been as far off the grid as possible.

Where was Clark then? Or Bryan White?

If they were involved like we thought they were, Allie might have had them arrested or at least removed.

The whirring of the elevator ceased as the doors slid open. I stepped off the lift into a hallway. A black woman in her 40s stood a few feet away. She wore a navy-blue business dress with a gold chain around her neck supporting an opal shining with flecks of pink and green.

"Mr. Gordon," she greeted me.

"Yes," I responded.

"Patrice Gray," she introduced herself. "I'm Ms. Tremblay's assistant. Why don't you come with me?"

"Was Ms. Tremblay expecting me?" I asked, feeling as if everything was in a set motion.

"She's told me if you showed up to escort you up immediately."

I let out a sigh. She couldn't reach me, so she waited for me to come to her. Had I been anyone else in the world, I might have called first. Although, I intended on confronting her brother-in-law; not find her raised from the dead.

"If you'll wait here," Patrice offered as she waved her hand toward a lounge area. "Ms. Tremblay is in a meeting, but as soon as she is available, I'll let you know. Can I get you a cup of coffee? Tea?"

"Coffee'd be nice," I agreed as I settled onto the black leather couch.

The side tables had a few industry magazines about logistics and transportation, along with a *Newsweek* and a *Bloomberg Markets Magazine*. I didn't think I could muster enough interest in any of the subjects to waste a few seconds flipping through the pages. My legs crossed, and I leaned back.

After almost an hour, Patrice appeared.

"Sorry to make you wait, Mr. Gordon," she apologized. "Ms. Tremblay can see you now."

I followed the woman down the corridor. She opened a door to usher me inside. As I stepped inside, the door closed behind me.

Across from me was an oak desk in front of a window overlooking the lake. A blond woman was working behind a computer as I stepped toward the desk. My eyes moved around the room, confused.

"Chase, how are you?" she asked.

"You're not Allie," I stated.

"Of course, I am," she insisted. The timbre of her voice was almost familiar.

I turned around, examining the office. Finally, I asked, "What the hell is going on?"

"I don't understand," she responded.

The door opened behind me, and I whipped around, prepared for an attack.

Alex Fretsh stood in the opening. "Chase, good to see you," he offered as he closed the door behind him.

"What in the actual hell is going on here, Fretsh?" I demanded.

"This is Allie Tremblay," he insisted.

"The hell it is!" I exploded. Looking back at the woman, I added, "A close replica."

Fretsh shook his head. "No, it's her."

"Where is she?"

"As far as anyone outside of this room is concerned, she is sitting behind that desk."

My teeth ground against each other. "Where is my Allie?" I snapped.

"Your Allie?" Fretsh asked with a smile. "How do you know this isn't the real Allie Tremblay?"

My head jerked back at the woman sitting poised behind the desk. "I know her," I insisted.

"Why?" Fretsh began. "Because you slept with her once after a night of drinking in the tropics? Or because she let you see how scared of water she was?"

I growled, "You have to be kidding me, right?"

"You knew a woman who claimed to be Allie Tremblay." Fretsh leaned back in his seat with a smug stare.

My head cocked a bit. "What are you saying?"

Fretsh shrugged. "I'm saying that you pulled a woman with no identification out of the ocean, and she told you she was Allie Tremblay."

"You're telling me it wasn't?"

"Chase, I'm not telling you anything," Fretsh explained. "Except this is Allie Tremblay."

I glanced between the two.

"Why don't we sit down?" he suggested.

There's a defense mechanism in many of us that puts us on a precipice, ready to fight. I was teetering on the lip. My muscles tightened. If the tide changed, I prepared to pounce.

But I lowered myself into a leather chair across from the fake Allie.

"Here's the deal, Chase," Fretsh explained. "The woman you rescued wasn't Allie Tremblay. In fact, it might be best to say you rescued no one."

"You replaced her," I noted. "How? Better yet, why?"

"None of that matters, really," he told me.

"Because a freight company is a nice under-the-radar delivery system for the CIA, isn't it?" I realized. "The Soria

Cartel was using it to deliver drugs. Why not let the US government use it to ship arms or money overseas? Hell, you already control the ports and customs, don't you?"

"Only in the States," Fretsh pointed out, matter-of-factly.

"Right," I quipped. "The CIA never gets involved in other nations' affairs."

"How did you do it?" I asked. "Other people knew Allie."

Fretsh shrugged with nonchalance. "Not really. She spent most of her time traveling. Most of the office staff dealt only with her father or brother-in-law."

"Clark," I announced with clarity. "What happened to Steven Clark? Or Bryan White?"

"Both of them resigned their positions. I hear they are taking a sabbatical in Honduras. I'm sure the government there might have some questions about what happened on Swan Island. Did you hear about that?"

"Classic government bullshit. You just make the people you want gone disappear?"

Fretsh laughed. "Is that different from waging a one-man war against an entire cartel? Pray tell, what did you plan to do if you found Steven Clark here?"

I fumed, but mostly because he had a point.

"I'm sorry about Ms. Tremblay," Fretsh acknowledged. "It was tragic, but at this point all those responsible are dead."

My head turned to look out the window. "Most of them at least."

"Cut yourself some slack, Gordon," he scolded. "You didn't do it."

My attention refocused on him. "What about her sister?"

"Sarah Clark is receiving the best medical attention. My understanding is she will probably never wake up, but she's going to be taken care of."

Looking at "Allie," I asked, "You're willing to give up your life to become someone else?"

The woman didn't flinch or reveal anything. She just stared at me.

"Allie would have smiled," I pointed out.

Fretsh commented, "Of course, this all falls under the auspices of national security, so I'll expect you to keep it to yourself."

"Who would I tell?" I asked. "You might swap them out."

As I pushed to my feet, I leaned over the desk. "You need to understand. I'm holding both of you responsible for Allie's sister. A spook like Alex here might be hard to find, but I promise I can track down the fake CEO of Banyan Freight."

"She's my sister," the faux Allie explained. "I will take care of her as long as I'm alive."

I grunted and walked past Fretsh.

"Chase, I might reach out to you sometime," he added. "If you ever want some work."

I twisted around to look at him. "Oh, you have my number?"

Fretsh grinned at my joke. "No, but I know where to find you."

I nodded. "My suggestion is you forget that kind of information. It might prove unhealthy."

The door hung open behind me as I passed the desk of Patrice Gray.

When I walked out of the Banyan Freight building, a few fluffy snowflakes were drifting down. The precursor to the coming storm. I found the Nissan Pathfinder I'd driven up from Mexico.

Four hours later, I crossed the border near Detroit. I drove through the night until I was in St. Louis, where I slept a few hours in the parking lot of a Walmart.

The rain complemented my mood. The next ten hours were a slog through the drizzle. The sun finally broke through the gloom around Valdosta, Georgia.

Outside of Orlando, I left the Pathfinder in the short-term parking at the Sanford Airport, where I bought a coach ticket to Montego Bay. By dusk, I was in a taxi taking me from the airport to the dock.

Carina floated, securely tied in her slip. While someone had searched her, she was in mostly ship-shape condition, minus a few bullet holes in her transom left from our late-night escape off Swan Island. They would wait a few days for repair.

I climbed aboard and found a bottle of Barrel Rum. After pouring a stiff shot into a tumbler with no ice, I sat at the settee and stared at the legs as they ran along the glass. After several seconds, I swallowed the contents in two gulps.

The empty glass rested on the dinette table as the halyards rang out against the mast.

Also By

For a list of other books by Douglas Pratt
visit the author's webpage at
http://www.douglas-pratt.com/